Look Back

to

Tomorrow

By Cherie' Waggie

PublishAmerica
Baltimore

ISBN: 1-60610-926-X
PUBLISHED BY PUBLISHAMERICA, LLLP
www.publishamerica.com
Baltimore

Printed in the United States of America

To Donna, Sevi, Marsha, and Faith, for their belief in me, and Mama, who gave me all of her talent. And for Bill, Marcia, Earl, Lawrence, and Terry for their inspiration and encouragement over the years.

Chapter 1

The knots that had twisted inside of Tao's stomach during what had been for him a grueling flight from New York City to Hong Kong finally relaxed as he stepped from the plane. He wasn't used to flying and he wasn't used to sitting still. The last 18 hours he'd spent on the plane that had been filled to capacity with people of all nationalities seeming to talk at once in their various languages, the closed confining space of the plane, and the uncomfortable seats, even though first class, had been nerve wracking for him. By the time the plane landed, his back and head felt as if there were firebrands burning though them and as he walked towards the terminal, he desperately wished for one of his pain pills packed in his suitcase.

He felt Lee's reassuring hand on his shoulder and glanced at his cousin. He knew Lee had been just as uncomfortable. He'd noticed the grimaces of pain on Lee's face during the long flight. When one passenger sitting in the seat next to him had accidentally tripped over his leg, Lee's face had actually gone white. Though healing, his legs were still very tender from surgery.

The year had been difficult for them and they had been warned not to hope for too much. The injuries they had each sustained drastically altered their lives, but their perseverance and stubbornness had paid off. They were both walking unaided.

Monica looked over her shoulder at Tao. She smiled, but he noticed the taletell look of concern on her face. She always knew when he was hurting. She waited for him to catch up to her then wrapped her arm through his as they walked into the terminal.

When Tao had last left Hong Kong, he had been 17 and returning from his parents' memorial service in China. He'd been in such a daze then he barely remembered the trip, let alone the airport. He didn't remember it being so huge, or so crowded. There were people everywhere. Like ants, they wound their way in a constant stream around and through the terminal, a kaleidoscope of every imaginable dress and nationalities. The claustrophobic feeling returned and all he wanted was to get out of the airport.

Sensing his discomfort, Monica squeezed his arm. There was a brief hesitation at customs when the agents came across the medication in his and Lee's bags, but they were ready with the proper paperwork to prove the prescription medicine was necessary.

The four were a family where once there had been none. Lee and Tao pulled together, determined not to spend their lives dependent on crutches of any kind. Officially on leave of absence, Tao had neither the inclination nor the desire to return to the San Francisco Police Department. Even before the shooting that had crippled his back, the 27-year-old Lieutenant Detective in the Homicide Division had considered retiring. The shooting only prompted him to take the final steps in giving it up.

Captain Greg Arama had assured him he still had a job, but Tao knew his injury had given the brass the excuse they had wanted to put him permanently behind a desk. He opted to use up the vacation and sick leave he had accrued during his eight years on the force, then retire permanently from the service on the disability pension the Department approved for him.

Lee's injuries had made it impossible for him to return to his 10-year career as Captain of the China Town Fire Department in New York City. Newly retired and fully compensated by the Service, he decided to return home to Hong Kong and asked Sophie to accompany him. She walked with him now, her arm through his, her head on his shoulder.

The women had no problems during the flight, except making sure their men were comfortable and not in pain. Sophie, a Registered Nurse, had kept enough medicine with her for Lee to take during the flight. The two of them had entertained themselves by watching the in flight movies, talking, and working the crossword puzzle books that Sophie had brought with her.

Monica and Tao had watched the movies as well, but Tao had been too restless to enjoy them.

The cousins had spent long hours discussing what they would do once they arrived in Hong Kong. Lee's parents, Meng and Kai Chi Wong, assured them they would have a place to live in the family home for as long as they wanted.

6

A prominent and prosperous self-made businessman, Kai Chi Wong diligently checked into many business opportunities for his son and finally found one they all agreed on. Together he and his brothers purchased a tour yacht on which Lee and Tao would conduct tours of Hong Kong and surrounding islands. The business would belong to them. Kai Chi and his brothers were simply investors.

Kai Chi and Meng waited at the Security gate of the airport. Meng, a tiny woman at 5 feet tall, in her 60's, her gray hair stylishly cut to frame her still pretty oval face, waved at her son and nephew as she caught sight of them and the beautiful blonde and brunette that walked with them.

Monica and Sophie were much the same in build, slender curved figures instead of the emaciated slimness that was so much the sought after and mostly unobtainable style. They were both the same age, the dark-haired, hazel eyed Sophie older by only a couple of months. Monica's Scandinavian roots were clearly evident in her bright blue eyes and long blonde hair.

Kai Chi, an older copy of his handsome son, athletically built from years spent as a fisherman and exercise from the Martial Arts when he was younger, stood at her side and offered his hand as Lee and Tao came up to them.

There had been estrangement between Kai Chi and Lee when he had decided to leave Hong Kong and move to America. Lee had hoped to locate his missing cousin from whom he had been separated as children. Time and circumstances postponed his plans until he chanced to see the news broadcast of the shooting that nearly claimed Tao's life.

Through that broadcast, Lee contacted and finally reunited with his cousin. Two years older, a little bit taller and heavier, Lee nonetheless was a perfect match in looks for Tao. When first reunited, Tao's thick black locks had been cut short due to the surgeries for the head injury he suffered in the shooting. Now, his hair grown out, he wore it similar to Lee's, down to his collar and framing his face. The two looked more than ever like twins, with almond shaped dark brown eyes, high cheekbones, deep dimples in their cheeks when they smiled, and perfect bow shaped lips.

It was too loud for anyone to say anything and be heard, so they didn't speak until they had made their way from the airport to Kai Chi's car. Tao and Lee dropped the bags in the trunk and then collapsed with Monica and

Sophie in the back seat of the silver luxury sedan that Kai Chi had driven.

They left the airport and drove through the busy, congested streets of Hong Kong. Again, Tao began to fidget at being cooped up inside a small space as they inched through the traffic. Despite the air-conditioned car, he felt as if he couldn't breathe.

Lee noticed the anxiety on his face.

"Take it easy," he said. "We're almost there."

"Take deep breaths," Sophie advised.

He did and it helped a little, but all he really wanted was space. He'd been shut up far too long.

The Wong home, situated on Victoria Peak, was a combination of modern western and traditional Chinese elegance, a rambling single-story house surrounded by sculptured Chinese gardens.

Lee and Sophie were shown to a wing of the house that would be theirs, as were Tao and Monica. It was then that Kai Chi told them of the family get together that evening.

Tao didn't feel like facing a lot of people so soon. He was too tired, in a bad mood, sore, and not given to being very sociable anyway, he wanted to spend the first evening quietly resting. Monica encouraged him to make the effort. She knew his reluctance was based partly on his fatigue and partly on his uneasiness in facing the family he barely remembered.

Lee was equally unenthusiastic. Sophie managed to talk him into it. He didn't like it, but agreed for her sake. Besides, he knew Tao would need the reassurance of his presence.

Tao stood by the window of the bedroom looking out at the sunset on the city that was both new and old to him. He heard the steady increase of voices coming from the main part of the house. He thought of the life he had left behind and the life he had come to. He was apprehensive. He wondered what life would be from that moment on and if he really wanted to know.

Chapter 2

Monica held his hand firmly in hers as they entered the main house. Close behind them, Lee led Sophie into the room where his Uncles waited.

Lee clapped Tao on the shoulder.

"Feels like a tribunal, doesn't it?" he whispered.

Kai Chi motioned them forward.

"Welcome home, Lee and Tao," he said.

He gave each of them a hug, then stepped aside to allow the two Uncles to offer their greetings.

The oldest, Kim Fong, scowled and stiffly hugged his nephews. Unaccustomed to being touched by anyone except Monica, Tao stiffened and noticed as he did, Kim's scowl deepened. As he stepped away, their eyes met and held for an instant with what felt to Tao almost like a challenge. He jerked his arm away and turned to greet the remaining Uncle, Keung.

Meng watched alertly. She had sensed Tao's uneasiness from the moment he had arrived and wanted to alleviate his apprehensions as much as she could. She had loved and grieved the loss of Kong and Tia and had offered many prayers over the years for the safe return of Tao. When Lee had called the year before with the news Tao was with him, she had felt those prayers were answered. When they had first met in the hospital in New York where Tao and Lee were patients, she had known immediately it would take time and effort on the part of everyone before Tao could again feel part of the family. She had warned Kai Chi against bringing the family together so soon, but he had insisted. Now she threw an annoyed glance at him as she came between Tao and Kim.

"The meal is ready," she said, guiding Tao to his seat at the table. "We eat first, talk after."

The rest of the family moved to their chairs and settled. There was general talk among the older men of various business ventures daily prospering. Listening intently without appearing to be interested, Tao began to relax a bit until he noticed that his cousins were staring at him. He didn't like it and kept his eyes averted as a precaution against losing his short temper.

The food on his plate was untouched. His injuries hadn't all healed. He had lost a partial sense of taste when the bullet that ripped through him damaged a nerve in his back.

Monica nudged him and nodded at his plate. Clearly uncomfortable, he kept his eyes down and took a hesitant bite. It tasted bland and unappetizing, which made him feel guilty, as he knew his Aunt had gone to a lot of trouble to prepare the meal. To make matters worse, he wasn't hungry.

Seeing his distress and embarrassment, Monica placed her hand over his and gently squeezed it. He smiled at her, then caught one of his male cousins staring at them with intent interest across the table. The young man had seen the exchange and the sneer on his face made it obvious that he wanted to know what it all meant. His invasion to their privacy made Tao angry.

Lee silently watched the exchange. He feared Tao would lose his volatile temper and prepared to step in. He was glad when, after a tense moment, Tao looked away. Tao was learning, but Lee knew it wasn't easy. Under different circumstances, Tao would never have given in and the outcome would have been unpleasant.

Tao's submission seemed, however, to encourage the cousin to take the matter further. With a malicious gleam in his dark eyes, he turned to his hostess.

"Auntie," he said, "the food is great. You've outdone yourself."

There was a general round of congratulations and praises at the table.

Tao felt the other man watching him, daring him, but he kept his eyes averted. One Aunt noticed his silence, however, and turned to him disapprovingly.

"Tao," she scolded, "you've not eaten. Meng has worked hard for your benefit."

He felt the rush of blood to his cheeks. Monica's hand again closed over his. All eyes turned to him. Conversation ceased. He stared at his plate. He knew his anger was about to explode, especially when he saw the sneer on the face of the young man. It was a dangerous moment.

Lee watched, his own anger radiating from him. Sophie held his hand under the table.

The family watched and waited for Tao's reaction. Forcing his temper down, he stood and turned to Meng.

"Forgive me, Aunt Meng," he said. "I'm sure the food is good, but I— have lost my appetite. *Dui m jue.*"

"Tao," Kim Fong's voice was sharp. "You embarrass your Uncle Kai Chi if you leave this room."

Astonished, Kai Chi turned on his brother.

Meng hissed at him, "Kim!"

Tao froze only for a moment then, ramrod straight, left the room. Monica excused herself and hurried after him.

Lee waited until Tao was out of sight before he stood and faced Kim.

"You've no right to say that!"

He faced his cousin.

"Don't ever humiliate him like that again."

"Lee," Kim ordered. "Sit!"

"This is my father's house, not yours," Lee said. "You can't order me around."

He left the room. Sophie hurried after him. In their wake, they heard Kai Chi angrily arguing with Kim. The entire family was in an uproar.

They found Tao and Monica in their suite. Tao sat on the end of the bed, his shoes off, his tie hanging loose around his neck, his hands dangling between his knees as Monica did her best to soothe his wounded feelings. When Lee and Sophie entered, he looked up.

"What did I do to deserve that?" he asked.

Lee shook his head.

"Nothing," he said. "That was Taibo, Uncle Kim's nephew on his wife's side. He's always been a troublemaker."

"I don't remember him," Tao said.

"You wouldn't," Lee said. "He was a baby when you moved to the States. His parents died in an influenza outbreak when he was a couple of months old. Uncle Kim raised him. Believe me, he's always been one to stir things up. He did that just to see what you'd do. I should've expected it and warned you."

He sighed heavily and jammed his hands in his pockets.

"I have a feeling they'll all try you, to see what you're made of. But don't worry, we're here and we're going to stand together, all four of us. They won't get away with it."

There was a soft knock on the door. Lee opened it, ready to battle with whoever it was. Meng stood holding a tray of food. He relaxed and took the tray, then stepped aside so she could enter.

"I know you're hungry," she said. "It's only rice and fish, but perhaps alone you'll eat better."

"*Dohje*, Mama," Lee said kissing her cheek.

He set the tray on the bureau.

Meng lifted her head with indignation.

"Kai Chi and Taibo have gone for a talk in the garden," she said. "Perhaps he'll learn he shouldn't prod the tiger."

Laughing at his mother's gentle defiance, Lee hugged her. She patted his chest and went to Tao. She lifted his chin so she could see his face.

"It was Taibo who embarrassed us tonight. Don't forget that."

She kissed his forehead and was rewarded by his shy smile.

"Why didn't you tell me about your problem? Even in New York you said nothing."

"Who told...?" Tao asked.

"Your doctor told Kai Chi," she said. "Your Uncle just told me. Now I understand why you stay so thin. You're family, Tao. You're now my son. Eat, and get some rest."

She left the room.

Lee closed the door. When he turned he was glad to see Tao was smiling.

Chapter 3

Lee rousted Tao out of bed before 6:00 for their morning run, a routine they had begun as their own form of therapy. They quietly slipped out of the house and set off at a steady pace through the nearly empty streets of the neighborhood where Kai Chi had built his expensive home.

The cousins said nothing as they kept stride with each other. Tao watched Lee's progress and after two miles, slowed his pace. They walked another mile to cool down. At the end of that mile, they turned and ran back to the house.

It was always the same distance. Every day, Lee pushed himself to go further. His legs were growing stronger. The scars were hardly visible, though he had to force himself to believe that. When he forgot, Sophie helped him remember.

Tao fared better. Though his back was permanently disabled, he worked hard at keeping his muscles strong and limber. He'd taken the role of trainer after Lee was released from the hospital.

At the house in the garden, he led Lee through their daily workout, stretching, toning, and strengthening their bodies until they were soaked with sweat. Two hours later, they were in the showers. They were dressed by the time Sophie and Monica were out of bed.

Some days, Sophie and Monica joined them in their run, but it was their first day in Hong Kong. Lee and Tao hadn't wanted to wake them.

Monica did some stretching before taking her shower and getting dressed. Sophie took her early morning workout in an entirely different way when she pulled Lee into bed with her. Soon the clothes he had just put on were lying in a pile on the floor.

Tao and Monica walked among the gardens. He loved it when she exclaimed over the scents, colors, and varieties his Aunt had lovingly planted.

She paused on the bridge spanning the brook to watch the large gold fish swim lazily through the clear water of a brook that cut through the center of the garden. Tao put his arm around her waist and pulled her close. He buried his face in her hair and drank in the fresh scent of her herbal shampoo. He kissed her neck. She turned and his arms slipped around her, pulling her into a deep kiss. The feelings she aroused in him and the fact he had given her the heart he had protected amazed and mystified him. Gently she pulled away and looked up.

"You better stop that," she said, "or we'll both be embarrassed."

He laughed.

Monica loved to hear him laugh. When she'd first met him, he'd been so deep inside of himself, so tormented that on their first night together, he'd cried as she held him. Her love broke through the barriers meticulously erected around his heart. Now he could laugh and smile, though it was still rare for him to do either. Still she knew he had miles to go yet, but they would get there together.

"When are you going to see the boat?" she asked, taking his hand and walking with him across the bridge and along the stone walk.

"We're supposed to meet Uncle Kai and Uncle Kim at eleven," he said.

She took note of his lack of enthusiasm.

"What are you thinking?" she asked.

"Uncle Kai gave Lee the keys to a car last night," he said. "It made me think of the old rundown jeep Ba ba and Uncle Kai bought from a serviceman returning to England. They were so proud because they owned a vehicle. It didn't matter how old it was. We kids thought it was the greatest thing to ride while other kids had to walk. Now Uncle Kai drives a fancy car and buys one for Lee—and a boat."

A light that Monica knew well crept into his eyes.

"What is it?" she asked, turning him to face her.

She encouraged him to talk about his parents, about his childhood. He seldom did. He never fully came to terms with the deaths of his mother and father. Their murders were never solved. For him there had been no closure. He'd told her that returning to Hong Kong made him miss them even more.

"Ba ba moved us to the States for a better life," he said. "He should've stayed here."

14

She touched his cheek.

"If he had," she said, "I wouldn't have known you."

He wrapped his arms protectively around her. Too well he knew that if his family hadn't moved to San Francisco, he wouldn't have been in New York City to save Monica from a killer.

Tao knew how much he needed Monica's strength to get him through the difficult nights when nightmares refused to let him sleep.

"What are you doing today?" he asked as they resumed their walk.

"Sophie and I thought we'd take a look at our new hometown," she said.

"Be careful," he said, "I know how the two of you are. You'll end up spending too much money."

"Oh pooh." She playfully punched his shoulder. "That's a sexist remark, Mr. Wong."

"But true where you're concerned," he said.

He sprinted away with her giving chase. They arrived at the house laughing and were met by Meng standing by the sliding doors.

Meng liked Monica. She was happy that her nephew had found someone to give him what he needed. The young woman was intelligent and levelheaded, able to keep Tao in check most of the time.

"Your breakfast is waiting," she said. "Lee and Sophie are already at the table."

She led the way into a different dining area than the one the night before. There was a traditional low table and pillows on the floor. A pot of rice and of tea sat in the center of the table.

Tao and Monica took their seats. Meng served the tea, then lifted the lid from the rice. The pungent fragrance of spices rose in the steam and made Tao's mouth water. Picking up his chopsticks, he took a small bite. He didn't know what Meng had used but the flavor was potent.

Meng kissed his cheek.

"From now on," she said, "you'll taste every dish. I won't allow anyone to embarrass you again."

She left them to their breakfast.

It was almost 9:00 when they finished eating. Monica and Sophie saw them to the door before getting ready for their day of shopping.

The car Kai Chi had purchased for Lee was a brand new convertible, white, with tan interior. Lee put the sleek little sports car through its paces along the winding streets of the city and pulled up in front of their slip at the pier just at 11:00.

Kai Chi and Kim were waiting for them at the gates and led them to the dock where the new yacht was moored. Neither Tao nor Lee had expected anything remotely like it. The sleek pearl white yacht gleamed in the sunlight.

"Well, what do you think?" Kai Chi asked.

"It's fantastic," Lee said. "Are you sure? I mean, I never expected this."

Tao walked the length of it, his hand drifting along the rail. He turned to his Uncles.

"I hope we deserve this," he said.

Kai Chi smiled at him.

"I've no doubts you and Lee will do well in this venture," he said. "Your Uncles and I have looked at countless yachts. This is the one we agreed upon. This is the one we know will bring you much luck."

Tao and Lee boarded. Kai Chi and Kim followed as they took a tour of the deck and went below to inspect the staterooms. The natural teakwood was polished to a high gloss. The staterooms would easily sleep six people. Genuine Corian countertops, recessed dual stainless steel sinks, finely finished teak furniture, cabinets, and dining tables left them open-mouthed.

"I don't know what to say," Lee said.

"You needn't say anything," Kai Chi said, clapping him affectionately on his shoulder. "I know this past year was hard for you. I want to make this year better. I know I can't replace the life you lost, but perhaps, jai, I can make your new one easier."

He paused. "And to make up for my foolishness."

Lee lowered his head in thanks.

"I'll do my best, Ba ba."

Tao was as grateful as Lee. He wanted to say something, but wasn't sure what. He started to thank Kai Chi, then caught sight of Kim. There was no friendliness on the man's face. Tao felt his defenses go up.

"*Suk suk*," he said, "Uncle, thank you from me as well. We'll use this gift to the very best advantage and make you proud."

Kai Chi was pleased. He'd been wary of Tao when he and Meng had flown to New York City to be with Lee during his first month in the hospital. Tao hadn't mentioned he, too, was a patient when he'd called. Spending time with him and seeing the genuine affection he held for Lee impacted the way Kai Chi felt about him.

Knowing it was Tao who, despite his own struggle with injuries, urged Lee to push himself, to not give up despite the pain and the predictions of the doctors made Kai Chi very fond of his youngest brother's son.

Lee caught the expression on his Uncle Kim's face. Protectively he placed his arm across Tao's shoulders.

"Let's see what else she holds," he said as he led him back on deck.

Chapter 4

Lee wanted to share his good fortune with Sophie and called her cell phone to give her the address of the pier. He didn't tell her why he wanted her to come, but urged her to hurry and to bring Monica. They arrived a short time later with Meng.

"It's beautiful," Sophie said as Lee helped her aboard.

Tao helped Meng then Monica onto the deck. Monica hugged him. Meng examined every detail as she walked about the deck.

"Shall we take her out?" Lee asked.

He couldn't wait to get his hands on the helm. It had been a long time since he had sailed a boat of any kind. His father and uncles had spent most of their youth working on fishing boats, making money for their families. Kai Chi had instilled his love of the sea in his youngest son and had often taken Lee with him.

After moving to New York City, Lee occasionally went with coworkers on weekend excursions or sometimes on chartered cruises. He'd longed for a boat of his own. His wish had been granted. Expertly, he guided the yacht into the channel.

The day was clear and the water was calm. He sailed around the edge of Hong Kong into the open sea before anchoring.

Anticipating that Lee would want to take the yacht out, Kai Chi had provided food and drink for the party. Meng, informed the night before of Kai Chi's plans, provided the spicy dishes.

Tao relaxed and enjoyed the cruise as he and Lee made plans for their first charter. They took notes and advice from Kai Chi and Kim about where the best courses for circumventing the islands were. Kai Chi was as enthusiastic as his son. Kim, however, said very little unless asked a direct question. His gaze drifted often to Tao, who noticed, but managed to ignore him. Nothing, he determined, was going to ruin the day.

Lee guided the yacht back to Hong Kong after lunch, comfortable with the feel of the helm. Kai Chi stood at his side. He'd missed Lee and regretted the harsh words they had exchanged the day Lee told him he was going to America.

Kai Chi looked to the deck where Tao and Monica sat tangled in each other's arms, dreamily watching the horizon. Tao was another of Kai Chi's regrets. He should have tried harder to find him. He hoped to let Tao know that he was very much a cherished part of the family.

Sophie, her face pink from the sun, joined Lee and Kai Chi on the bridge. "How's it going, skipper?" she asked.

Lee drew her to his side. "This is more than I could've hoped for," he said. "Ba ba, I really do appreciate you helping Tao and me in this."

"I'm glad to do what I can," Kai Chi said. "There's much yet to do, but I know you and Tao can handle the business from here on. I don't think you'll have many problems with charters. Tourists are plentiful."

About that, Lee had no doubts. He had seen the piers teaming with people waiting for the ferries and other charter boats. Hong Kong was a living city 24 hours a day. He and Tao would need to sit down and create a schedule of hours for operation, concessions for special charters, and so many other things. It would certainly keep them busy.

When he reached the pier, he maneuvered the yacht smoothly into its slip. Everyone pitched in to clean up. Everything shut down, they disembarked and walked as a group to the cars. Once there, Monica, Sophie, and Meng gave them news they had been keeping to themselves all day.

"We've found an apartment," Sophie said.

"Well, with help from Meng," Monica interjected.

"It's big enough for all four of us," Sophie said. "We thought we might start out that way, all of us living in one place until we're more established."

"It's a converted warehouse," Monica said. "The building is four stories and on each floor there are four apartments. The one we looked at has three bedrooms, two with bathrooms, a huge open living area, and a kitchen. The four of us will fit without any problem and still have plenty of room left over."

"There's a fantastic view of Hong Kong through sliding glass doors that lead out to a balcony," Sophie said.

Tao and Lee had no objections. They just hoped they could afford it. There had been much discussion about where they would live before they left New York. Living in Hong Kong would be expensive, even for a small apartment or flat. They decided to share expenses until their business was on firm ground. The apartment the girls found sounded like what they needed and was probably very expensive.

"How much?" Lee asked.

His mother punched him lightly in the arm and frowned at him.

"Don't worry," she said. "I wouldn't suggest it if it was too much. You can afford it."

Kai Chi was about to protest until Meng dug her elbow into his ribs. She wanted her children to live their own lives, not feel like guests in the home of their parents. Kai Chi didn't like the idea, but knew Meng's stubbornness and didn't argue. Tao and Lee would want their own homes.

He was surprised to see Kim standing silently to one side scowling. Kim had been acting odd all day. A serious man, he seldom smiled, but his severe behavior of the past few days was rare even for him.

"What's bothering you?" Kai Chi asked.

"I'm not sure of this," Kim said, his eyes fixed on Tao. "I know I agreed to help Lee, but Tao is unknown to me. I remember Kong Lee too well. He had no sense. I have to wonder what kind of man Tao is. If he's anything like his father, he'll be a hindrance to Lee's success."

Kai Chi set his jaw. Kim and Kong had never gotten along very well. Kong had resented his elder brother's attempt to control his life. Kai Chi believed it was the reason Kong had decided to leave Hong Kong. He felt it unfair for Kim to doubt Tao when he knew so little about him.

"You're being unfair, Dai Goh," he said. "Tao's nothing like Kong Lee and if he is, so what? Tao's life has been lonely and isolated. There's not been anyone to ease his grief."

"That was his decision," Kim said. "I gave him a chance to remain with us when he brought Kong and Tia's ashes to the family shrine. He refused."

"Tao was only 17," Kai Chi said. "He asked for our understanding and help. Instead you told him to leave. In that, he is like his father. He refused to be dictated to."

He watched his nephew speaking quietly to Meng and Lee by the cars.

"I believe he'll be good for Lee and Lee for him," he said. "They've shown they're capable of overcoming obstacles. Look at their progress this past year."

He faced Kim squarely.

"In the hospital Lee told me how Tao nearly died in the shooting in San Francisco. And Lee would have died if Tao hadn't carried him out of the fire. They're good for each other and they'll do well. Don't place extra burdens on them with your unreasonable doubts."

He turned away. Kim wasn't a sympathetic or sentimental person. Even so, Kai Chi felt better having said his piece.

Tao watched as Kai Chi approached, but it was Kim who held his attention. Kim was watching him and he didn't like it or the way Kim silently nodded to himself before getting in his car and driving away. Tao remembered how, at their last encounter, Kim had made him feel like a mongrel pup begging shelter from a storm. He didn't like Kim, then or now. He wouldn't be bullied.

Monica touched his arm, breaking his thoughts.

"Don't let him bother you," she said. "You're much more than he'll ever be. You don't have to prove yourself to anyone."

"How'd you know what I was thinking?" he asked as he kissed her cheek.

"I've been watching your Uncle since this morning," she said. "He hasn't taken his eyes off of you. It makes me uneasy."

"We're just strangers to each other," he said. "It'll get better."

He said it, but he didn't believe it.

Meng and Sophie were making plans for the apartment when Tao and Monica rejoined the conversation.

"Shall we go see the apartment?" Sophie asked.

The women and Kai Chi loaded into Lee's car. Lee, having noticed the silent exchange between Tao and Kim, held back for a moment.

"What's wrong?" he asked. "Between you and Uncle Kim?"

"Nothing," Tao said. "I just have a lot to learn, I guess, about family."

Lee knew there was more to it than that. The problem was his Uncle not Tao.

21

Tao opened the passenger side door and started to get into the car when he caught sight of someone standing on the boardwalk. His and Taibo's eyes met. Taibo casually flicked his cigarette into the channel and, with a sneer, sauntered away.

Following Tao's gaze, Lee saw Taibo leaving. There was no need to say anything. He knew, as well as Tao did, that trouble was brewing. Taibo wouldn't be satisfied until he repaid Tao for whatever Kai Chi had said to him the night of the dinner. And, Lee reflected, causing Tao trouble would be a big mistake on Taibo's part. As Meng had said, it wasn't wise to prod the tiger.

Chapter 5

By the end of the week, they were in their new apartment and their belongings began arriving from storage in the States. It wasn't long before Sophie and Monica were arranging everything to their liking.

Lee and Tao were kept busy obtaining permits, licenses, and other official documents they needed to operate their tours. They spent hours working out the schedules and operating hours when they weren't acquainting themselves with the yacht. Their first tour was already scheduled for the first of the coming week, which gave them the weekend to relax and enjoy their new home.

Saturday, Monica and Sophie decided they all needed a break and insisted on shopping for things for the apartment. Lee pretended to wince whenever Sophie purchased something and teased her about single-handedly supporting the Hong Kong economy.

Tao contributed by taking charge of dickering. He was good at it, which surprised the other three.

That night they went dining and dancing. Sophie noticed towards the end of the evening that Lee was limping.

"I don't know about you," she said, "but I'm exhausted. I think it's time to go."

Tao seconded the idea. He had been monitoring Lee, too.

At home, Sophie shooed Lee into a hot bath, then gently massaged his legs and feet. He was sound asleep by the time she finished.

As she watched him, she remembered the first time she'd seen him in the hospital. It was only two days after the fire. He'd been heavily sedated against the terrible pain from the burns. She was instantly drawn to him and remembered thinking he was the most handsome man she'd ever seen.

She'd fallen in love with his sweet nature and humor that miraculously survived despite his devastating injuries.

All of his nurses declared him to be their most favorite patient, but it was she who had found the special place in his heart. Whenever she entered his hospital room, he brightened. They had spent hours talking, especially when Lee couldn't sleep. It was during these talks she'd learned of Sophia, who he had rescued from a fire then had fallen deeply in love with, only to discover that she was running from the same killer who had nearly killed Tao in San Francisco. The killer, Arturo Gravelli, had set fire to Sofia's house and left an unconscious Lee to die.

Sophia mysteriously vanished at the end of the case. Lee assumed it was into the Federal Witness Protection Program. Arturo turned out to be the brother of Saleno Gravelli, California's most prominent syndicate leader. Ironically it was Saleno who rescued Tao from the explosion Arturo set to kill him.

When Sophie first met Tao, she'd expected him to be like Lee, since the two looked so much alike. But unlike Lee, Tao was a difficult, uncooperative, stubborn patient, traits that turned out to be his strongest assets. He refused to let what the doctors said keep him and Lee from pushing their limits toward a complete recovery. His determination and tenacity impressed Sophie, even though at times his tantrums wore on her patience. Still, she couldn't help but love him. Without Tao's courage and sheer cussedness, Lee would never have defeated his own crippling injuries.

She kissed Lee's cheek before curling close to him. His warmth and the steady sound of his breathing lulled her to a peaceful sleep.

Tao and Lee were up early Monday for their daily run before breakfast. They ran their usual five miles and headed back to the apartment. Monica and Sophie watched from the balcony and waved as they returned. None of them paid any attention to the car that suddenly roared to life, and with a squeal of tires, tore up the street like a black projectile directly at Tao.

Monica screamed. Sophie called out a warning as Lee grabbed Tao around the waist and heaved him out of the way, but not before the handle of the car door struck Tao on his right thigh.

He cried out as he and Lee tumbled to the ground. He managed to roll free at the last minute to avoid crushing Lee under him. Lee scrambled to him as he clasped his hands to his injured leg and gritted his teeth against the pain.

"Lie still," Lee ordered. "Lie still. Let me see."

He pried Tao's hands away so he could take a look at how badly he was hurt.

Monica and Sophie reached them. Monica cradled Tao's head on her lap as Sophie took control of the emergency.

Tao held Monica's hand while Lee and Sophie examined the ugly red welt forming on his upper thigh just below the hem of his running shorts.

"There's no break in the skin," Sophie said. "That's good. But you're going to have a nasty bruise and your leg will be sore."

He grimaced as she gently prodded the area around the injury.

"It just swiped you," she said. "But maybe you should see a doctor."

"No!" Tao almost shouted the word.

The last thing he wanted was to see any more doctors. He'd had his fill of them over the past year.

"That car meant to hit you," Monica said.

Lee had the same thought.

A small crowd of people gathered around them and several hands reached out to help Tao to his feet. They asked him if he was alright. He put his weight on his leg, found he could stand, and assured them all he was fine.

Lee questioned the crowd for possible witnesses but no one offered any information. Not surprised, he helped Monica assist Tao into the apartment.

A hot bath was Sophie's recommendation, then an ice pack afterwards since Tao insisted on being so stubborn. Monica ushered him into the bathroom and left him to soak in the bathtub.

Sophie argued with Lee that he should call the police.

"Believe me," he said, "that's not a good idea. Tao's not hurt badly. If he wants to call the police then I'll leave that to him."

"But that car tried to run him down," Sophie said.

"We think," Lee said. "We have no proof. I didn't see it. Tao didn't see it. Did either of you?"

They both admitted they weren't positive they saw the car until just before it struck Tao. It could have been an accident. The driver might have lost control of his car, and frightened he'd hit someone, just driven away.

"Just leave the matter be," Lee said.

"Maybe someone saw something," Sophie said.

"I doubt it," Lee said.

"But…" she protested.

"Sophie," he said, "this isn't New York City. Even there, you wouldn't find many people willing to step forward and admit seeing anything. Let it go for now."

"I don't understand you, Lee," she said. "This isn't like you."

"I'm not turning my back on this," he said. "I think that car was aimed at Tao, but I can't prove it. If I ever see it again, I'll recognize it and whoever is driving will have some explaining to do."

Monica returned to the bathroom to check on Tao. She was still shaken and angry.

"Maybe you'd better not go out today," she said.

"The charter's already been made," Tao said, standing up and wrapping a towel around his waist.

He limped over to the bed and sat down.

"I'll be okay."

His eyes were angry. Monica knew arguing with him would be a waste of time. She helped him dress in a pair of cutoff denim shorts, a tee shirt, and his deck shoes. He limped into the livingroom where Sophie handed him the ice pack to place on his thigh that was now turning a deep shade of purple.

"You gonna be able to make it?" Lee asked. "I can manage alone."

"I'm fine," Tao said. "Stop fussing over me."

At the yacht, he forgot all about his sore leg as he and Lee prepared for their first tour. Their customers arrived at 11:00, eight people wishing to spend the day fishing and seeing the islands around Hong Kong.

The day was warm. It wasn't long before Tao shed his shirt. Lee sidled up to him.

"Better put that back on," he said. "We're not in California."

The passengers didn't seem to notice, but he did as Lee suggested.

They took turns at the helm while the tour entertained. It wasn't necessary to participate, which didn't bother Tao. Serving as Security, he did keep a close eye on the guests, mostly to make certain they didn't fall overboard.

At 3:00, they turned for home and arrived at the slip at 6:00. The passengers, having enjoyed themselves a bit too much, disembarked, over enthusiastically thanking Tao and Lee before teetering up the pier.

"How's your leg?" Lee asked as he and Tao cleaned up the mess left behind and prepared the yacht for the next tour.

Tao had forgotten all about his injury. He examined his thigh, which was still tender and nearly black, but it didn't hurt as much as it had that morning.

Lee sat against the rail of the deck and crossed his arms.

"Who do you think it was?" he asked.

Tao said nothing.

"You know this is serious," Lee said.

Tao found a place next to him.

"Taibo's a punk," he said. "I'm not afraid of him."

"Maybe you ought to be," Lee said. "This is Hong Kong. Taibo is probably a gang member, maybe even a Triad. It's no minor matter."

"And I'm no minor matter either," Tao said. "I'm not stupid, Lee. I've dealt with his kind for years. I know what to do."

He stood up and stared out across the channel.

"He better keep his distance."

Chapter 6

They arrived home late, hungry and in good spirits from a successful first day. Dinner waited on them. The day was humid and hot. Before they finished their meal, it began to rain.

Monica opened the sliding glass doors to let in the fresh air and breeze. Tired and a little sore, Lee plopped down on the couch after he and Sophie washed the dishes. She massaged his shoulders and neck and soon found herself seated on his lap with his arms wrapped around her.

Monica placed some pillows in front of the window and lay in Tao's arms watching and listening to the gentle shower of rain. The rain and the whispers of the couple on the couch soon lulled them to sleep.

When she woke, she and Tao were in bed. He had wakened and carried her to their bedroom. It was dark and raining harder. She heard thunder and cuddled next to him. He tossed, turned, and mumbled in his sleep. Propping on her elbow, she touched his face. It was hot and sweaty, as was his body. This was one of the difficult nights. She smoothed his hair from his forehead and spoke soft soothing words until he quieted and opened his eyes.

"Bad dreams?" she asked.

He nodded.

She kissed him and his arms slipped around her to pull her tightly against him. She massaged his chest.

"It's a miserable night," she said. "It's so hot and humid, it's a wonder you're sleeping at all."

"You're not," he said.

"No," she said, "for the same reason. I didn't know what the weather would be like here. Is it always this way?"

"I don't remember," he said.

He didn't remember what the weather was like or anything else about

28

Hong Kong other than the many, many people. It was as if nothing began until the day his parents died.

"It's all as new to you as to me then," she said.

She laid her head on his chest and listened to his heartbeat.

"Umm," he mumbled as his arms tightened around her.

They were quiet for a long time and she thought he had drifted back to sleep until he whispered, "Don't ever leave me."

She sat up to search his face. The tears on his cheeks caught her by surprise.

"What is it?" she asked. "Your dreams?"

He nodded.

"What were they?" she asked, kissing the tears away.

"My parents," he said.

She knew how much their memories hurt him. The more time she spent with him before they married and especially after, she encouraged him to let go of the past. He had never allowed himself to grieve, never gotten over the rage. She, Meng, and Kai Chi had spent hours with him after he left the hospital getting him through each stage of grief, anger, guilt, until all that remained was acceptance. Tao couldn't accept the death of his parents. There were too many unanswered questions.

"Tell me," she said.

"It was hot, like now," he said. "Mama was behind the cash register. Ba ba was stacking boxes in the back when the men came in. He heard them demand the money and ran into the store."

The foggy vision battled to clarify in his mind. Shadowy figures moved through gray light. He struggled to see the blurred faces.

"I was helping Ba ba in the back. He ran into the store and I heard the gunshots. I heard—Mama scream. I started to go in. There were—men— in the store. One of them held Mama on the floor—before he shot her, too."

He paused to take several deep breaths.

"They didn't see me. I ran and hid in the freezer where the police found me. I couldn't talk. The doctors said it was from trauma. The truth was, I didn't understand a word they were saying. I didn't speak or understand English."

Monica felt the ragged intake of air through the palm of her hand on his chest.

"I never told any of them; no one except Mama Kim, my first foster mother. I don't remember telling her, but I must have. The police came and asked a lot of questions. She had to interpret for me. When they left, she explained why it was so important I remember. But everything went dark except the nightmares."

Monica wrapped her arms around him and pulled him as close as she physically could. No child should witness a horror like he had. She wished he didn't have to remember, but knew it was imperative for him to finally face it and put it behind him forever.

Chapter 7

There were two tours every day and Lee was able to make a good financial report to his father the first week.

Acting as mechanic and security, Tao kept the yacht in running order and a keen eye on the passengers. He and Lee poured over manuals, yachting books and magazines, articles, anything they could get their hands on to learn everything about their new business. There were nights the girls went to bed alone while the cousins hovered over the materials. Sophie and Monica grew used to waking and finding them asleep at the dining table. It took much working out and massages to ease the cramped muscles.

Lee went to the slip early, leaving Tao to run errands. There were several mornings he arrived at the pier to find Kim's car in the parking lot and Kim watching them from the window of the small restaurant overlooking the pier.

It was Lee's opinion that their uncle was observing their progress. He was the largest investor and wanted to make certain his money had been invested well.

Tao had other ideas. He hated the scrutiny, especially when he often caught sight of Taibo lurking around the slips. It wasn't concern for his investment, but something else, something Tao couldn't figure out, which brought Kim to the pier. Seeing Taibo hanging around increased his uneasiness and on those days, he paid extra attention to his daily inspections of the yacht before it set out.

Meng was often at the apartment helping Sophie and Monica decorate. She brought some of the things she intended for Lee to inherit as well as items she found in markets here and there.

Monica and Sophie loved having the older woman with them. They suspected Meng's visits were because she had no daughters.

Despite her age and demeanor, Meng was agile and active. She spoke her mind when she thought prudent but in such a way that it sounded wise not scolding.

Sophie's mother had died when she was a teenager. They had been close and the loss had been difficult for her. She found in Meng a renewal of that relationship, the ability to share everything from her deepest secrets to idle gossip, to laugh and have fun, and most of all to share the love they both felt for Lee.

Monica, on the other hand, had grown up in a farming family. Her father had been the authority. His judgements and orders were never challenged, not by his children and never by their mother. Monica felt her mother a submissive mouse who never stood for what she thought was right. Her father had given an ultimatum to his daughters if they didn't follow his rules, they could leave his house. Her oldest sister had left, married the local banker, and started her own family. The next oldest left right after high school graduation and had become a successful real estate broker in their hometown.

Monica's ambition had been to go to New York City to attend college, majoring in acting and dance. When she approached her parents with her plans, her father had forbidden it, had informed her that she was to get married and settle down to be a proper wife. His choice of her husband was her ex-boyfriend, a boy she had known all of her life. Her father had known and had been friends with the boy's parents for years before either he or she was born. She had briefly dated him, but discovered he was overbearing and possessive like her father. Even after they broke up, he was often at the farm, always acting as if she was still his. She had done everything to let him know she wasn't and never would be interested, which made him all the more determined to hang around.

The night before graduation, she had secretly packed her bags, written letters to her two younger sisters, still in grade school, and after the graduation ceremony, had slipped out of the house when everyone was asleep. She had emptied her savings account, an inheritance from her grandmother and what she had earned as a carhop, and had gone by bus to New York City. She enrolled in college, worked her way through by working part-time as a waitress, won her degree and several small roles in a few plays, and lived contentedly enough, certain that she would eventually acquire what she'd dreamed of all her life.

The night she met Tao, everything had changed.

Being married to him and being with his family brought her a sense of belonging she had never known. Meng and Kai Chi had taken Tao in as if he'd always been their own, and had welcomed her with no reservations as a beloved daughter-in-law.

Meng was a guide, teacher, and interpreter when they were out. She was funny, intelligent, a willing listener, a gentle heart, and knew all the best places to buy what they needed.

Monica found that especially helpful when choosing things for Tao.

There was one particular market that Meng loved to frequent. It was tucked away in a corner of the city that seemed to be caught in time. Old Hong Kong lived and thrived on the dusty streets lined with open booths and markets, a step back into its history.

"It's the best place to buy vegetables and find rare spices," Meng said on their first excursion.

Monica and Sophie followed her through the market as she pointed out the different herbs and spices that held the strongest and most pleasing flavors. Dutifully, Monica bought them on Meng's promise of recipes for her to try out on Tao.

Booths of silks and brocades, gold and silver, everything old and new imaginable kept the women busy. Sophie reminded them of what Lee had said about their spending and they agreed he might well be right.

They were having such a good time, they hated to go home, but by lunchtime, they were footsore and breathless. Meng took them to a quiet restaurant and found a corner table where they gratefully dropped into the seats. They trusted her to order the meal. They paid no attention to the rest of the customers until a shadow fell across their table.

Meng's smile instantly turned to a frown of disapproval.

"Auntie," Taibo said. "How nice to see you."

"If that's so," she asked, "then why have you shadowed us without greeting all morning?"

Monica and Sophie were surprised by her question. They hadn't seen him.

Monica didn't like the look of the four young men standing directly behind Taibo. They were all dressed in dark jeans, white tee shirts, and black leather jackets. They leered at her and Sophie.

At her side, Sophie appeared disgusted and annoyed more than anything else. Monica knew she was biting her tongue.

Taibo offered Meng a condescending grin as the pulled a chair around and straddled it.

"I'm impressed, Auntie," he said. "You're very observant. I didn't want to ruin your outing."

"I don't care for your impression," Meng said. "And I'm not your Aunt. This is a private meal and you're being disrespectful."

Unruffled, Taibo rose. His friends did likewise. Monica felt a little frightened. She wasn't worried for herself. Her thoughts were on Tao's parents. It was believed to have been a gang that killed them. Tao hated gangs.

"I'll let you ladies return to your meal," Taibo said.

He winked at Monica, which made her want to slap him.

"I hope the rest of your afternoon is enjoyable," he said.

He nodded for his friends to follow him and left the restaurant.

Meng angrily shoved her food away. Monica and Sophie had also lost their appetites. The morning was ruined.

"Why didn't you tell us they were tailing us?" Sophie asked. "I didn't see them. I guess I'd better start paying attention to what's going on around me."

Meng was disappointed for the other two women. She had enjoyed their company.

"I didn't want to spoil our outing," she said. "I had seen them earlier, but paid no attention until I saw them again. I have been watching them closely, but they were keeping their distance. I will have a talk with Kai Chi about this."

She saw the girls home. She had missed having daughters. Her older sons and their wives lived in other countries. She hardly knew her daughter-in-laws. Now, she had two. She corrected herself, not quite. Monica was as close to a daughter-in-law as she could be, but Sophie...

Meng considered Lee and Sophie's relationship and wondered who was dragging his or her feet.

The purchases put away, Sophie fixed some tea and they sat quietly in the livingroom. All three were upset about the way the way the afternoon had turned. If Tao and Lee were to discover Taibo had been following them, Meng knew it would lead to trouble.

The door to the apartment opened abruptly and Lee entered supporting Tao, one arm draped around his shoulder. Both men were soaking wet. Tao's face was gray with a tinge of red on his cheek and jaw.

Monica hurried to help him to the couch.

"What happened?" Sophie asked.

She knelt in front of Tao and took a good look at his face. His eyes were clear, which was a good sign. She took his pulse and sent Lee for her emergency bag.

"Nothing," Tao said, gritting his teeth.

Meng brought him a towel and wrapped him in it after Monica pulled off his wet shirt.

"The rain made the deck of the yacht slick," Lee said as he set the bag at Sophie's side.

Meng gently wiped the back of Tao's head with the edge of the towel. It came away with traces of red.

Sophie carefully examined the small cut above the surgical scar. It was only a small cut.

"It was raining hard when we started back. I told the passengers to stay in the stateroom," Lee said. "They were drinking and one of them came on deck anyway. We pitched and he went over the rail. Tao caught him and was trying to get him back when the man's idiot friend shoved Tao out of the way. Tao almost lost his grip before they could get hold of him, then did lose his grip and went over when the yacht took another pitch."

Monica grabbed Tao's hand. He gave her hand a reassuring kiss.

"I managed to get Tao onboard," Lee said, "but his feet slipped out from under him and we both hit the deck."

Tao sucked air through his teeth as Sophie cleaned the cut on the back of his head and daubed antiseptic over it.

"It's not serious," Sophie said. "Head wounds always bleed a lot. You'll live."

She looked at Lee. His cheek beneath his right eye was purple and there was a cut above his lip. She glanced at his knuckles. Both were black and blue.

"You next," she said, pulling him into a chair. "What's the other guy look like?"

Lee ducked his head in embarrassment.

"He won't be chartering another one of our tours, I guarantee it," he said. He winced as Sophie doctored his wounds.

"You're both soaked," Meng said. "You better get into dry clothes. I have to go. Your uncle will hear about this."

"Mama, don't," Lee said, walking her to the door. "I'm sure they're not the only problems we'll ever have."

He kissed her cheek. She didn't answer him as she left.

After Meng had gone, Sophie headed Lee to their bedroom so he could change.

Monica pulled Tao to his feet and herded him into their room.

Tao pulled his wet clothes off as soon as the door was closed. He'd just stepped out of his jeans when Monica's arms came around his waist and held tight.

"What's wrong?" he asked.

"You could've been killed," she said.

"It's just a bump on the head," he said.

"You fell overboard," she said. "You could've drowned."

"Could, but didn't," he said.

He led her to the bed and they sat down.

"If Lee and I are going to run this business," he said. "we have to accept the risks. This is one of them. I'm a strong swimmer. It's okay."

"I guess I can't put you in a glass house," she said. "But Tao, I worry about you. You've been through so much this past year. I don't want to lose you before I've had a chance at a life with you."

He slid his arms around her shoulders and pulled her into a deep kiss. His skin was damp and hot. She ran her hands over his back and shoulders, loving the feel of him.

Together they lay on the bed, her cradled beneath him. He'd never known love like hers and hungered for it. She was everything to him and he had to fight the fear every day that she might stop loving him, might stop wanting him, might stop needing him. If she ever left him, he didn't know if he could go on.

"Tao," she whispered as she felt the tension in his movements.

"Don't ever stop loving me," he whispered into her neck.

Each time she heard those desperate words, her love for him grew stronger. She knew about his fear, even though he didn't know it.

"I won't," she said.

She pulled his body into hers, as close as she could bring him, and held on with all her might.

Lee sat on the bed while Sophie doctored his cheek, lip, and hands. He flinched from the sting of the antiseptic, which caused her to shake her head in grim amusement. She took a towel and dried his hair and body. He was ticklish and squirmed as she ran her fingertips across his ribs.

She closely examined his legs as she dried them, marveling at the miracle of medicine that allowed only one or two small scars to show after all the skin drafts. He'd told her the best thing about the burns was his legs weren't hairy any longer.

"What do you see down there that's so interesting?" he asked.

When Sophie looked at his legs, it sometimes frightened him that she might find something wrong. The memory of the months in the hospital was still vivid. He had no desire to repeat those days and nights of misery.

Sophie, her eyes directly in line with another part of his anatomy, raised her eyebrows at him. She leaned her hands on his knees and, with a sultry smile, licked her lips as she reached for him.

Chapter 8

It was a little after seven when the phone rang.

"*Wei?*" Sophie answered the way Lee always did.

"Sophie?" It was Meng and she sounded upset.

Sophie sat up and glanced at Lee. He was still asleep and hadn't heard the phone.

"Yes," she said. "What is it?"

"Kai Chi just arrived home," Meng said. "I haven't had a chance to tell him what happened and he's very upset. He said a man from the tour this morning came to his office and said the boat wasn't safe. He wanted his money back."

"That stupid man," Sophie said. "Is Kai Chi there? May I speak to him?"

She waited until Meng handed over the phone to Kai Chi.

"Lee told us the passengers were drunk," Sophie said when he answered. "Lee said it was raining and the sea was rough. Those men didn't stay below like they were told"

"I checked the weather," Kai Chi said. "The sea was very rough."

"One of the passengers fell over the rail," Sophie said, "Tao caught him, but got knocked over before he could get him in the boat."

"Over?" Kai Chi's voice had taken a concerned note. "How over?"

"As in over into the sea," Meng said at his elbow, "and he bumped his head. Lee pulled him to safety and, from the looks of it, got into it with one or both men."

There was a long silence, then Kai Chi chuckled.

"Yes," he said, "the man did have a black eye and puffed lip."

"I don't know what he's trying to pull," Sophie said.

"Don't worry," Kai Chi said. "I'll take care of it. Are Lee and Tao okay?"

"Yes," she said, "they're fine. Worn out, but fine."

There was a long pause. When Kai Chi spoke again, he sounded disappointed.

"Oh. I was hoping you would come for dinner tonight. I have guests coming. It's a good time for prospective tours."

"Kai Chi!"

Sophie bit her lip when she heard Meng's scold. Meng was arguing with him in Cantonese. Sophie couldn't follow what she was saying, but knew Kai Chi was getting an earful.

Kai Chi's dinner parties would be a good place to advertise the tours known. He did know a lot of influential persons.

"I'll check with the others and let them get back with you," she said.

Meng stopped talking, probably having left the room in a tiff. She had known how tired Lee and Tao were when they got home. Sophie would be willing to bet that Kai Chi hadn't told her about his plans to invite them.

"Good," he said. "Dinner is at nine."

Tao fidgeted with his tie as Lee drove them to his father's. Monica finally slapped his hands away and tied the bow tie herself. She straightened it with a final pat.

"There," she said. "What are you so nervous about?"

She had an idea. He didn't like being around a lot of people, especially strangers. And he didn't like wearing his monkey suit as he called it. Kai Chi had told them it would be a formal affair and the invitation had come at short notice, passed on to them by Sophie after their nap.

Lee was just as uncomfortable, but more used to going to formal functions than his cousin. As Captain, he'd attended many dinners and ceremonies.

Dressed in their new gowns, the girls had received appreciative whistles when they'd made their appearance before leaving the apartment.

Lee groaned as he pulled into the circular drive behind a line of cars.

"Valet parking," he said. "I was hoping this wouldn't be that big of a deal."

He wouldn't have come if Sophie hadn't insisted it was a good chance for potential charters. Even at that, he didn't like the idea. He was too tired and his face was black and blue from the fight. She used her make up to hide what she could, but he was very conscious of the damage.

"Relax," Sophie said. "It'll be a good chance for you and Tao. I'm sure there are plenty of business people who'll take advantage of the tours."

Lee shook his head. He was proud that his father and uncles had prospered during their lifetime. But sometimes, he felt they flaunted their wealth too much.

He turned the keys over to the Valet and then led the others into the house. There were many people dressed in both western and eastern finery, mingling with drinks and hors d'ovres. Tao visibly shrank back and Lee knew he was claustrophobic as soon as they walked through the door.

"Take Tao out to the patio," he said. "I'll get us some drinks and be there in a moment."

Sophie caught hold of Tao's left arm and Monica took his right. They walked with him to the patio and the fresh air. Away from the crowd, he relaxed.

"Maybe we should've stayed home," Monica said as they sat down on the low stone wall around the edge of the patio.

"No," Tao said. "I agree with Sophie. It's a good chance to meet some possible clients and investors. I'm okay. I'm just—not used to all of this."

She kissed his cheek. She much preferred small parties to grand affairs herself.

Lee returned with their drinks.

"I ran into Ba ba," he said. "He was glad we're here, but too busy right now to say hello. I told him we'd be out here."

He sat down on the other side of Sophie. There were traditional Chinese lanterns bathing the garden in soft light and a warm breeze. He placed his arm around her and held her.

The music began, a slow, intimate rhythm that added dreaminess to their surroundings.

Monica pulled Tao to his feet and placed her arms around his neck. Her head against his shoulder and his arms wrapped around her waist, they started dancing.

Lee and Sophie followed their lead, drifting in slow circles around the patio.

Tao opened his eyes to gaze at Monica when a movement at the patio doors caught his attention. He stopped moving. Feeling his tension, Monica pulled away and looked up. His eyes were fixed on the doors behind them. She turned.

Lee saw Tao's expression and stopped dancing. His expression mirrored Tao's. Sophie and Monica stared at the small, slender woman with perfect Oriental features and long, shiny, straight black hair standing in the open doorway, her eyes riveted on Tao.

Monica touched Tao's arm as he pulled away from her. His expression changed from stunned disbelief to anger. Without a word, he disappeared down the garden walk. Monica started to follow, but Lee held her by the arm. He shook his head.

"Let him be," he said. "This wouldn't be a good time."

Monica looked to the door, but the woman was gone.

"Who was she?" she asked.

Lee took a deep breath and let it slowly out.

"Lei Ling," he said.

Monica didn't know what to do. She looked to Sophie who was just as confused. Lee excused himself and warned them to stay put while he went in search of his parents.

"I'm going after him," Monica said, glancing into the garden. She was worried about Tao.

"Stay here," Sophie advised. "You don't know where he went."

"I don't care," Monica said. "I have to find him."

She headed down the walk searching for Tao in every shadow and praying that he hadn't left the grounds to walk home.

In the house, Lee spied his parents and angrily confronted Kai Chi.

"Ba ba," Lee said as he pulled his father to one side. "What's going on?"

"What?" he demanded, pulling away from Lee's grip.

"Why did you," Lee said, "invite her here like that? Don't you know how much that hurt Tao?"

"*Mai y ai?* What are you talking about?" Kai Chi asked again.

"Lei Ling," Lee said. "Why is she here? Who invited her?"

His parents glanced at each other then at him. Kai Chi scanned the room.

"Where is she?" he asked. "Are you certain? Did you see her?"

"Yes, I saw her," Lee said. "More important, Tao saw her."

"Calm down," Kai Chi said. "And keep your voice down. I didn't know she was here. I'm not the one who invited her."

"*Duh m jue,* " Lee said ducking his head. "I'm sorry. I didn't mean that. I was just wondering why she was here. Maybe you have some idea?"

"Are you sure it was Ling?" Meng asked. "You only saw her once, at the wedding, and that was years ago."

"I have their wedding picture," Lee said. "I know what she looks like. And Tao knows—he saw her first."

"Do you see her now?" Meng asked.

Lee looked across the sea of faces until he spied her standing next to the patio window.

"There,"' he said, pointing her out.

Meng and Kai Chi looked. It was true. The young woman standing by the window looking into the gardens was Lei Ling. Meng remembered all too well the beautiful young girl in her white wedding gown standing stiffly next to a nervous Tao. Meng had known then that Tao's marriage would never be happy. The girl obviously didn't love him. Meng had wanted to warn him, had considered it, but at that point in his life, Tao wasn't listening to anyone, especially the family he thought had abandoned him.

Her heart went out to her nephew. Such an unhappy child; such an unhappy man, until he found Monica.

"I'll see what I can find out," Kai Chi said. "Go to Tao. Make sure he's alright."

He drifted into the crowd, casually mingling among his guests. Lee figured he would subtly pry information from them until he discovered who had brought Ling.

Meng placed her hand on his arm.

"Monica?" she asked.

"In the garden, with Sophie," he said. "I asked them to stay there."

"*Tao hai bin do*? Where is he?" she asked.

"In the garden somewhere," Lee said.

"*Daan duk*? Alone?" Meng slapped his arm. "He shouldn't be alone. *Hui. Faai di*. Go. Find him and go home. This party wasn't a good idea for you. I tried to warn your father, but he wouldn't pay attention."

She gave him a little shove and he hurried out.

Sophie came instantly to her feet as he returned to the garden.

"We need to find Tao and leave," he said. "I shouldn't have let him go off alone. This is a disaster."

He looked around.

"Where's Monica?"

"She went to find Tao," Sophie said.

He moved down the path. She quickly followed. The garden was dark. The moon and lanterns offered little light by which to see. Lee didn't want to call out. He scanned the shadows and saw the outlines of other couples, but didn't see Tao and Monica. He was about to suggest going back for help when they suddenly appeared on the path in front of him.

"What are you doing?" Tao asked.

"Looking for you," Lee said. "We're leaving."

They circumvented the house and waited while the Valet brought the car around. The drive home was made in silence. Tao stared out the window. Monica wanted to help, but wasn't quite sure how to deal with this situation.

At the apartment, he went directly to the bedroom. When she went in, she found him sitting on the edge of the bed staring into space. One of his shoes was on the floor, one sock still in his hand. She kissed the top of his head, then undressed and climbed into bed. She didn't know what to say.

Tao shook himself out of his thoughts and finished undressing. He slid under the covers and lay on his side. Monica had found him near the little bridge in the garden. She'd said nothing, just stood next to him watching the fish. Having her at his side had made him feel less pulverized, but he was worried that she might be angry. He couldn't blame her. Seeing Ling had resurrected old pain. It wasn't fair to Monica to be subjected to that. He wanted to know why Ling had been at the party and who was responsible for her being there. He didn't believe that Kai Chi would invite him knowing Ling would be there, or visa versa.

"I'm sorry," he said aloud.

"What?"

Monica sat up and turned on the lamp. He rolled onto his back. She kissed him, then lay down close to him. He kissed the tip of her nose. She ran her hand along his shoulder and arm until their hands found each other.

"Tell me how you felt," she said.

"Angry," he said. "Surprised. Terrified."

"You don't still love her, do you?" she asked.

"No."

He said it with such vehemence that she laughed.

"I know," he said, "what I thought I had with Ling. I was only 17 years old, too young and too alone. I was reaching for anyone. I thought she loved me. Stupid."

"It wasn't stupid," Monica said. "It was normal. Teenage boy with a beautiful teenage girl—the only difference was the circumstance. She wasn't your first girl, was she?"

He studied her a long moment before he answered. Satisfied that she was only curious, he shook his head.

"I was a normal enough teenager," he said. "I had a couple of girlfriends in high school. After graduation, they went to college and I went to China."

He was silent for a long moment.

"I wasn't a sweet child. After being taken from Mama Kim, I had trouble adjusting anywhere else. None of the other foster parents could handle me, or that was their excuse."

"What did you do?" Monica asked.

"I ran away from a couple of the homes," he said. "But it didn't do me any good."

He sighed and ran his hand through his hair.

"My Social Worker hated me," he said. "I don't know why, but she did. The feeling was mutual. She kept putting me in the homes of people who were only fostering for the money."

He turned to Monica when she gasped.

"Some of the families had one or two foster kids. We were put on strict schedules, not allowed to go out, not even on the weekends while their own kids were given free rein."

"What did you do?" she asked.

"Nothing, mostly," Tao said. "Except run. I always went back to Mama Kim. The Social Worker knew where I was and always came after me. The man and his wife in the last home I was in liked to make people think they took me in out of kindness. They liked to show me off to their friends—the poor little orphan they had rescued."

"How old were you?" she asked.

"Fifteen. Almost sixteen. They had a son. He was a nice kid. I found out later it was because he already knew what I was about to find out."

Monica touched his cheek. He kissed her hand.

44

"I was told to come home immediately after school every day. I had to do my homework as soon as I got there. By the time I was done, it was time to eat. After I finished eating, I was allowed one hour of free time, then had to take my shower and go to bed."

Monica was horrified.

"What happened?" she asked.

"I wouldn't do it," he said. "I had baseball practice after school. I wasn't going to let the team down because of some hypocrite. I told him so. He didn't like it and warned me not to disobey him again."

"But you did," Monica said.

"I did," Tao said. "He got in my face that time and locked me in my room. I went to baseball practice the next day."

"What did he do?" she asked.

"He came to my room and informed me I was going to do as he said. Then he knocked me across the room. I landed on the floor. It was the only chance I gave him. I was on my feet and in his face before he could take a breath."

"What did you do?" Monica sounded worried.

"I told him that was the last time he would ever hit me," Tao said. "He must have believed me because he left the room and locked me in. I crawled out the window and ran off."

"Did you go to Mama Kim's?"

He shook his head.

"The cops picked me up before I could get there. They hauled me off to Juvenile Detention. The next morning, I went before the judge. No one was there, not even my Social Worker. I started throwing up, so the judge called a recess and had me taken to his chambers to lie down. Sometime after that, Mama Kim came. The judge placed me in her permanent custody until I was 21."

His expression softened and a smile crossed his lips.

"I had been in 7 foster homes in less than two years. I was glad to be back at Mama's. I found out later that my Social Worker had been removed from my case. I don't know why, and I didn't care."

Monica cuddled next to him. He held her tight and felt better. The shock of seeing Ling had placed barriers in his way. Those barriers had to come down. As he drifted off to sleep, Tao smiled ruefully. He hoped Monica never came face-to-face with Ling.

Chapter 9

The following weeks proved to be busy for the yacht tours. The weather remained mild and the tours went out twice daily, one in the morning and one in the evening. The night of Kai Chi's party was forgotten as Lee and Tao focused their minds on business. On the third week, a wedding excursion was booked and was the only day that it rained.

The happy couple and their relatives assured them the rain simply added to the special memories of the day.

Kai Chi found out that Ling was the wife of the only son of a business associate. That associate brought his son, recently a partner in his father's company, to introduce him to important business contacts also attending the party. Ling's appearance was purely accidental.

With Monica and Sophie running the administrative end of the tours, keeping records, taking reservations, and so on, the cousins were free to focus solely on the actual tours. There were no more mishaps, the groups more tightly screened, and Lee posted a list of specific rules for the passengers to follow.

Tao was seldom seen above deck. Lee piloted the yacht as if born to it. Life took on a semblance of normalcy for them. On the days the tours didn't run, their time was spent fixing up the apartment. There was plenty of space to fill.

The warehouse had been converted into four apartments on each of the four floors, all spacious, a rarity in Hong Kong and not inexpensive. The Wongs knew they were fortunate their business was turning out to be so lucrative.

Kai Chi kept a close eye on the bottom line of the financial aspect. He invested heavily in the venture, confident that his youngest son would prove just as successful as his two oldest sons.

He was proud of Lee. At 23, Lee had become one of the most outstanding firefighters and paramedics in Hong Kong. This won him the chance for a position in a newly formed international firefighters exchange program. He had been eager to take the offer. Kai Chi had vehemently opposed it, especially when Lee announced his choice for the exchange.

Kai Chi had done his best to talk Lee into going to Australia instead. Lee refused. His mind was set and Kai Chi knew the motivation was the missing Tao. Lee had always been a fierce protector of his almost twin. A cave in when the boys were younger had sealed their relationship. Lee had dug his six-year-old cousin out before Tao suffocated. Nights after, only Lee could comfort Tao from the terrible nightmares that followed. The loss of Kong and Tia was painful. Not finding Tao was too much grief to bear. Kai Chi knew Lee thought he didn't care. In truth, he was trying to spare him. Tao was gone and there was no getting him back.

After their quarrel, Kai Chi found it hard to let Lee know how proud he was of him. Letting him go had been hard, but Kai Chi had many friends in New York City, business associates and colleagues who kept him apprised of Lee's career.

All their differences disappeared the night he received Tao's unexpected phone call from the hospital. A fire had nearly claimed Lee. The rift between them had to be mended before it was too late. There might not be another chance.

Tao's call had surprised him in more ways than one. He hadn't been aware that Tao was with Lee. He had found Tao a bit of a trial at first. He hadn't known what to expect. Tao had failed to mention he, too, was injured. But the belligerent, angry way Tao fought not only the doctors and nurses, but for his and Lee's life touched Kai Chi's heart. He recognized the defenses his nephew had erected around him were his way of surviving. After only a few minutes standing at his bedside watching him in restless sleep, Kai Chi had decided the lonely, tortured young man would never feel forgotten again.

It was Kim's behavior toward Tao that perplexed Kai Chi. As eldest son of the family, Kim took the role of Patriarch after the untimely death of his father. He pushed his brothers, Kai Chi, Keung, and Kong with conviction that they succeed.

Kong was determined to get away from Kim's tyrannical thumb, to meet success on his own terms. The two had quarreled over his decision to go to America. Kim had turned his back on him. Kai Chi had been torn between the two. He hadn't wanted Kong to leave, but didn't condemn his decision.

Keung openly supported his younger brother. The quiet one in the family, the mediator, Keung was like their mother, able to smooth over ruffled feathers and hurt feelings with quiet words and clear thinking. He had said little about the tour venture, though he willingly invested, but he kept his distance. Unlike Kim, Keung offered his nephews breathing room. He didn't want to stand over their shoulders. He knew success wouldn't come from overshadowing. All this he had confided in Kai Chi when he had attended the first financial meeting with his brothers three weeks after the tours began.

Tao was glad things were coming together, but Taibo's lurking at the pier every morning rankled him. Taibo never tried to keep his presence a secret, but did keep his distance. Tao knew if either of them approached the other, it would be a losing battle for one of them. But it was with greatest restraint that he turned away from the temptation.

He wasn't the only one who regularly saw Taibo. Sophie and Monica often caught sight of him watching the apartment or following them through the markets. His presence made them nervous. They weren't sure what he might do, but as long as he didn't approach or threaten them, they wouldn't tell Tao or Lee. There was no telling what either of them would do.

Kai Chi secretly recruited Monica and Sophie to help him in planning Meng's 60th birthday. They wanted it held on the yacht and they enlisted Tao and Lee's help with the decorations and catering.

What began as a simple private tour soon grew to include more people. Lee kept careful tally as each name was added. The yacht accommodated only so many.

The day of the party, Lee, dressed in white Dockers, a short-sleeved white dress shirt, and white sneakers, was on hand to greet the guests arriving around eight in the morning.

Dressed in an identical blue outfit, Tao saw to the drinks as Monica and Sophie served as hostesses, mingled with the guests, and served the hors d'ovres.

It was Monica who spotted Taibo watching her and Sophie. His eyes traveled the length of her body and made her feel as if touched by something vile. She made her way to Sophie's side as quickly as she could and whispered in her ear. Sophie looked around until she saw him deep in a discussion with another guest.

"Try to keep Tao from seeing him," she said. "If he does, he's liable to toss him overboard."

"Would that be such a bad thing?" Monica asked.

She was only half joking.

Sophie agreed that the idea had merit, but said nothing as she gently shoved Monica to go find her husband. She, in turn, went to find Lee.

There was no love lost between him and Kim's nephew and he might well be as tempted as Tao to feed Taibo to the sharks.

It was a difficult game of hide and seek throughout the morning, but Monica managed to keep Tao occupied and from seeing Taibo. Despite Sophie's best efforts, Lee spied him about noon.

She saw him tense and following his gaze, she saw Taibo near the stairs. Taibo was watching Tao, who was several feet away, as far from the crowd as space available allowed him to be.

She slipped her hand into Lee's. He glanced at her.

"You knew he was here, didn't you?" he asked.

She nodded.

"Well," he said, "I guess I can't make him walk the plank."

He set his jaw and let the matter go. Taibo was, after all, family, too.

Chapter 10

The mission to keep Tao and Taibo apart seemed to have been successful. The girls kept the guests entertained while Lee was busy at the helm. None of them had seen Tao for a couple of hours since Lee saw him go to the engine room.

Lee thought the best thing they had done was to take to the sea. Tao genuinely seemed to enjoy keeping the yacht purring under his care. He was living instead of plowing headlong down a course of self-destruction.

The long talks with Detective Bryson Royo and Bryson's partner, Emily Sconey Royo, had been Lee's first introduction to Tao's life. According to Bryson, work was all Tao knew, all he did, all he thought about. He was a good cop, the best, but it had come with a terrible price. He had no other friends, had always been a loner hungering to belong yet keeping everyone at arm's length.

A loud bump beneath his feet startled him out of his thoughts. Angry muffled voices came through the ventilation shafts. They were coming from the engine room.

Tao worked his way to his private sanctuary in the engine room. As much as he wanted to join the celebration for Meng, there were too many people on deck. He was glad it hadn't rained. He liked the hum of voices and music mingling with the hum of the machinery. It created its own music.

"Nice boat, cousin."

The familiar mocking voice spoke from behind him. He felt the fires start to burn through his veins. He turned to face Taibo leaning easily against the door, arms crossed, looking smug.

"They went all out for the two of you," Taibo said.

Tao didn't answer. Taibo straightened. Tao tensed.

"You don't talk much, do you?" Taibo asked.

He moved to Tao's right. Tao's eyes never left him.

"You were a cop," Taibo said. "Nearly got you killed from what I hear. Still could if the wrong people knew."

Tao knew he was being baited. He didn't like it. But he knew his could not be the first attack.

"You know you're running into trouble, don't you, cousin?" Taibo asked.

He took a couple of steps towards Tao. Tao readied himself. Taibo stopped with less than a foot between them.

"You don't know what you're into," he said, "and if I were you, I would walk very softly."

"Leave," Tao said.

There were times when the peculiar rasp to his voice was very effective.

"Or what?" Taibo asked.

Tao closed the gap. He was shorter and leaner than Taibo, but equaled him in strength. He snatched fistfuls of Taibo's jacket and pulled him close.

"You don't want to find out," he said and flung Taibo away from him. "I don't know what your problem is, but you better back off."

Taibo stumbled but stayed on his feet. He ran at Tao. Tao was waiting for him and met him with two solid punches to the chin and gut. He sidestepped Taibo's follow through.

"*Chut hui!*" he ordered. "Get out!"

Taibo didn't listen. He charged again. The two were both trained in martial arts from an early age, but Tao was a champion, conditioned and disciplined. He met the charge and drove Taibo out of the engine room. They crashed through the doors just as Lee reached the deck. Several women screamed as the combatants landed on the deck. Tao rolled and managed to get to his feet as Taibo sprang to his. They were breathing hard.

Taibo came again. Tao was ready for him, but Taibo managed to block the blows. He swung at Tao. Tao ducked under him and kicked back, catching him in the side. Taibo stumbled, whirled, and pushed forward to let his momentum carry him into Tao. They both flew backwards.

Lee and his cousins moved in to separate the two men. Keung and two of his sons tried to catch hold of Taibo as Lee did his best to grab Tao. They managed at last to snag both men and hold them away from each other.

Lee held Tao by the shoulders. Tao's lip was bleeding and he had a nasty bruise on his cheekbone. His knuckles were bleeding. Monica and Sophie examined the damage and did what they could to wipe the blood away.

Kai Chi demanded to know what the fight was about and who started it.

Tao's left lung had never regained its full strength. He was breathing hard and unable to answer. Lee worried that if he didn't concentrate on regulating his breath, he would start coughing.

Taibo struggled against the hold his Uncle and cousins had on him. Keung glared in the direction of Kim who stood silently to one side stoically watching.

Taibo swiped at his mouth with his sleeve and pointed a finger at Tao.

"You're gonna regret this," he threatened. "We aren't finished yet. By the time I get done with you, you'll wish you'd stayed in America."

Tao tried to pull away from Lee's grip.

"Calm down," Lee said.

"What's the matter, Tao?" Taibo taunted. "Going to let someone else do your fighting for you?"

"That's enough," Meng said, stepping between them.

She turned to Taibo.

"You have caused enough trouble."

"I haven't even started," Taibo said.

Tao lunged forward, but Lee grabbed him around the waist and held him.

"Tao, stop it," Lee said. "Don't let him get to you."

Tao wasn't listening.

"Come near me again," he warned Taibo, "or any member of my family and you'll be the one who'll be sorry."

Lee had eased his hold on Tao. Keung and his sons had released Taibo, who seemed to have quieted. As soon as they stepped away from him, he moved as if to turn.

Tao saw the knife drop from Taibo's sleeve into his hand. He shoved Lee out of the way and twisted to one side just as the knife flew past him. It grazed his shirt as it went by and over the side of the yacht. Before it hit the water, he grappled with Taibo's other hand before the second knife could be thrown. They flailed back and forth, trying to overpower each other.

The other men moved in again as Taibo turned Tao's back to the rail and drove him into it. Tao planted his feet against the deck. His deck shoes kept him from sliding as he pushed against Taibo's attack. Taibo pressed forward to push him over. Tao sidestepped him and Taibo's momentum carried him over the rail instead of Tao. As he went, he grabbed Tao's shirt and they both ended up in the water.

Everyone ran to the rail as Lee and his cousins stripped off shoes and shirts and dove in. Lee swam to Tao who had been shoved under by Taibo.

Tao kicked and caught Taibo in the stomach. Taibo involuntarily gulped a mouthful of salt water, spat it out, and lunged at Tao again. By that time, Lee had grabbed Tao around his chest and swam hard to separate him from Taibo.

Tao fought to knock Lee's hands loose and kicked to keep Taibo at bay. Lee knew Tao was out of control, felt the rippling fury as it boiled out. Tao had been aptly nicknamed *Tiger*. He growled and spat like the big cat. It was all Lee could do to hang on to him.

The other cousins managed to capture Taibo, but had as much difficulty holding him. Taibo finally broke away from them and dove. He grabbed one of Tao's legs and pulled him under out of Lee's grip. Both men were doing their best to keep each other from gaining the surface.

Taibo locked his hands around Tao's neck. Tao slammed his fists onto Taibo's arms trying to break the hold. He kicked, landed solid blows on Taibo's hips and ribs, but Taibo held on.

Tao was suffocating. His old terror overcame him. He fought wildly, scratching, kicking, punching, but in the blows were ineffective in the water.

His lungs were about to burst. He had to breathe. Before he made the fatal mistake of gasping for air, he was jerked above the water. He sucked in the life giving breath as his head broke the surface.

Lee had him around the chest again and towed him towards the yacht. "Take it easy," he said. "Relax. I've got you."

This time Tao allowed him to take over. He was too tired to resist. When they reached the yacht, helping hands reached to pull both of them onboard.

Tao was eased to the deck, coughing and spitting up what water he had swallowed. He heard the commotion behind him as Taibo was hauled out and carried a safe distance away. Tao looked where Taibo sat hunched over, gagging and coughing up water.

Monica and Sophie brought blankets to place over their husbands' shoulders. Meng hovered close by.

"What the hell was that all about?" Lee demanded between breaths.

Too winded to speak, Tao shook his head. He wasn't sure and he was too tired to care. Taibo had deliberately prodded him into a fight, but why was a mystery.

A shadow fell across him and he looked up. Kim stood directly over him. There was nothing friendly in his gaze. With a snort of disgust, Kim turned and went to Taibo. He knelt on one knee and spoke quietly to his nephew. Taibo nodded several times then Kim left him.

Lee and Kai Chi watched when Kim came and were as confused by his behavior as Tao when he left. They helped Tao to his feet, then Kai Chi went to speak with his brother.

Lee, Sophie, and Monica helped Tao to a stateroom. He and Lee kept reserve clothes onboard for emergencies, and Lee handed him some dry clothing from a cupboard in the room. He went into the lavatory to change while Monica took his wet clothing and folded them into a plastic trash bag Sophie handed her.

When Tao emerged a few minutes later, Monica sat him on the bed and lifted his chin. Bruises were forming on his neck from Taibo's deadly grip.

"Are you alright?" she asked.

Her fear and worry were visible.

He nodded.

There was a knock on the door. Lee admitted Kai Chi, Keung, and Meng into the room.

Kai Chi was angry and wanting explanations.

"Where's Taibo?" Lee asked.

"They took him forward," Keung said. "We thought it best to put distance between these two."

"Wise decision," Meng said.

Kai Chi glanced at his wife then turned to Tao.

"I don't know what this was about," he said, "but be careful. It's evident Taibo is very dangerous. Your Aunt has told me..."

He flinched from the elbow dug into his side. Meng shook her head. The warning came too late.

"Told you what?" Tao asked.

"Nothing," Meng said. "Only that Taibo appears dangerous. You must be careful, Tao."

"He'd better be careful," Tao said.

He looked up.

"*Dui m jue,* Aunt Meng," he said. "I'm sorry. This was supposed to be your special celebration. I turned it into a disaster."

Meng hugged him then placed her hand on the side of his face.

"You're not at fault, Tao," she said. "Don't worry."

She kissed his cheek before latching onto her husband's wrist and nearly dragging him from the room. She was speaking low and rapidly to him as they left.

Lee, Sophie, and Monica sat with Tao. Sophie and Monica both knew what Kai Chi nearly said and were glad that Meng had stopped him. If Tao found out that Taibo and his friends had been following them and Meng, there would be another fight.

"You need to rest," Sophie said. "Stay in here. We need to get back to the guests. I'll bring you two something to drink."

Lee squeezed her hand.

"I better get out of these wet things and head us home," he said. "Take it easy, Tao."

When they were alone, Tao apologized to Monica.

"I'm sorry," he said.

She sat with his hand in hers.

"It's not your fault," she told him, her eyes on their entwined fingers.

She didn't sound totally convinced.

"Why didn't anyone tell me he was onboard?" Tao asked.

"Because we were afraid what happened would happen. Taibo was looking for a fight. He's been watching you all day, waiting for his chance. I'm sure of that. Be careful, Tao. That snake is up to something. I feel it."

He sighed heavily and placed his arms around her. She leaned her head against his chest, feeling safe in his arms.

Chapter 11

When they reached the slip, Tao went to tie up while Lee saw to the departing passengers. Kim and his sons stepped from the yacht with a sullen Taibo among them.

"Watch over your shoulder, Tao," Taibo shouted. "I'm coming for you."

Kim grabbed him by the arm in warning then propelled him toward the dock.

Tao started forward, but was blocked by Lee's arm.

"Settle down," Lee said. "That's what he wants."

Tao stayed but didn't let the threat pass.

"Anytime," he shouted back.

"Tao!" Lee said.

Taibo glared back and spat on the ground. Tao's gaze didn't waver as he watched him leave. He was aware of Kim watching the exchange between them. Taibo wouldn't back off. Tao wasn't afraid of him. He wasn't afraid of Kim either. He didn't know the catalyst that had started Taibo's hate campaign against him, but he had a feeling Kim was behind it. It didn't make sense, but he wasn't going to let either of them intimidate him.

That night was a bad one. He tossed and turned, restless and unable to unwind. When he did drift off to sleep, the nightmares haunted him until he woke.

Monica did her best to comfort him. She massaged his back and attempted to make love to him but he couldn't relax. As much as he wanted to love her, to hold her, he couldn't settle his mind or body.

"I'm sorry," he finally said. "I think I'll go in the other room."

She watched him pull on his jeans. His mood concerned her, especially after the incident on the yacht.

"Tao?"

He looked at her and in the gray light of their room she saw his restlessness etched on his tired features.

"Bad night," he said. "I'm sorry. Go to sleep. I'll be okay."

He wandered into the livingroom and sat on the floor by the window. Hong Kong stretched out below, the many lights testimony to the constant life teaming on the streets. He thought about the San Francisco streets. Life went on there, too, at night, but it was different, darker, more menacing.

He had lived on those streets, lurked in the shadows and watched in the darkness. His life had been those streets. What remained were the nightmares, the black dreams that crept into his mind to remind him of the ghosts he left behind.

"Tao, *mat ye si a?*"

Lee dropped into one of the chairs. He hadn't been able to sleep either and heard him. He knew he was having a difficult night.

"What's up?" he asked again.

"*Ngoh m ngaan fan,*" Tao replied, his voice muffled in his arms resting on his knees. "Not sleepy."

Lee knew it wasn't true.

"Want to talk about it?" he asked.

Tao shook his head. Lee waited.

"I came here," Tao said after several minutes, "to start a new life not repeat the old one. I don't want trouble, but if it starts, I won't back away."

Lee sighed and ran his hand through his hair. It was as he suspected.

"I don't know what Taibo's problem is," he said, "but if he doesn't ease up, you won't be alone. I apologized to Mama, but she said it's for Taibo to do, not us."

He shifted in his chair and sighed.

"You want something to drink?"

He didn't wait for an answer. He went to the kitchen and returned with two glasses of orange juice. He pressed one into Tao's hand.

Lee listened to the night sounds and found himself thinking of his New York City apartment.

"I don't think we'll go out today," he said. "We're not booked and it'll give us a day to do some work around here."

There was no response. Tao sat with his knees drawn up and his head resting on his arms.

"Tao?"

"Umm?"

Lee leaned forward and tapped Tap's arm.

"Hey," he said. "Bed."

Tao lifted his head, his eyes heavy with fatigue. He shook his head and stretched out on the carpeted floor.

"Too restless," he said. "Keeping Monica awake."

Lee handed him a pillow from the couch and covered him with the throw.

"*Jo tau, Sai Lo,* " he said. "Goodnight."

He returned to his own bed. He watched Sophie as she slept and thought how beautiful she was, how much she meant to him. Like Tao, he had bad days when the pain was too much. The memory of the fire repeated itself over and over in his dreams. He never talked about those dreams to anyone but her.

He stretched out on the bed and stared at the ceiling. His mind drifted to thoughts of Sofia. He wondered where she was, if she was well. How long did it take to recover from the horror she had suffered? He'd asked that question a million times, about her, about hundreds of others. He felt he might know a little better now, from his own experience, from Tao's. Tao was still recovering from all he had been through. A year wasn't enough.

Sophie snuggled against him and nestled her head in the curve of his shoulder.

"Where were you?" she asked with a sleepy yawn.

"Talking to Tao," he said. "Bad night."

"For everyone," she said, her mouth against the skin of his neck. "He okay now?"

"He's asleep," he said. "I hope he'll stay that way. He's so restless, he went into the livingroom so he won't bother Monica."

"Why is he so unsettled?" she asked, her lips tracing a path from his shoulder to the hollow of his throat.

"Too many ghosts," he whispered.

He wrapped his arms around her. She kissed his chest then his abdomen.

"If you don't stop that," he said, "we'll not get very much sleep."

She raised herself on her elbow to look at him.

"Are you sleepy?" she asked.

The damp cold bit into his face and arms. Sweat ran along his face and neck. Salt stung his tongue. There was ice on the wall where next to where he crouched. He felt their presence, knew they were there, watching, waiting. He had to get past them, to reach the yacht moored at the dock.

He felt his heart pumping, heard the breath in his chest. His gun held ready, he slowly counted to three and darted from his hiding place.

Bullets flew around him like angry hornets. He felt the first sting his shoulder. He stumbled, but kept running. The yacht lay just ahead.

On deck, a woman reached for him. He almost touched her fingers when he felt the second bullet rip through him and worm its way out of his chest. He fell into the icy water. Unable to breathe, he struggled for the surface. Shadows bobbed all around him, bumping into him.

One of the shadows bumped into his arm and floated into view. It was a body. They were all bodies, white and dead, and he knew their faces—too many faces.

In terror, he forced his head above the black water. A hand reached for him. He looked into the face of the woman on the yacht. Instead of helping him, she pushed him under and held him there. He was unable to break free of her grasp. Panic overtook him. He screamed.

"Cheryl!"

He sat up gasping for breath. Pain shot through his back into his head. He doubled over, held his temples and felt the heat of sweat on his face.

"Take it easy."

Lee's soothing voice found its way through the throbbing in his head. He knelt next to him, his supporting arm around his shoulders. Sophie had her medical kit and was busy taking his blood pressure and pulse. Monica handed him his medication.

Lee helped him onto the couch.

Sophie went to brew the herb tea that always seemed to help while Monica massaged his shoulders. He leaned forward on his elbows. He felt very hot.

He accepted the cup of tea Sophie handed to him and to the others. He used it to wash his pill down.

"Talk about it?" Lee asked.

Tao shook his head.

"You cried out for Cheryl," Lee said.

Tao rubbed his stinging eyes.

"I know."

"What happened?" Lee asked.

Tao looked into the faces of the three people he loved most and was reassured. The dream had been too real. He shivered as he repeated it to them.

"I don't think any of us are qualified to psychoanalyze Tao's dreams," Sophie said. "It's just a dream, a collage of memories. Don't let it upset you."

She was right. They were just memories. They couldn't harm him.

"I think," Monica said, "we should all go back to bed. All of us—to our own beds."

She took Tao's hand and steered him to their bedroom. He felt better. She, Lee, and Sophie were his strength. He was thankful they were in his life.

She had him lie on his stomach and pulled off his jeans. With soft gentle fingers she massaged his back and neck. She leaned over him and kissed his cheek. Her hair brushed his face and he blew it out of the way, then sneezed.

He buried his face in his pillow to stifle his laugh and felt her shaking against him as she, too, tried to keep from laughing out loud. She kissed him between his shoulder blades then on his neck. She nibbled at his ear. He rolled over to catch her in his arms.

"Don't do that," he said. "You know what happens when you do."

"Umm," she murmured seductively, snuggling against his chest. "I do."

She tickled his ear again.

Chapter 12

The four of them slept late. When they woke and dressed, Sophie and Monica put the men to work moving, lifting, and fixing things they had been unable to. They had been working all morning and were ready for a break when the phone rang

In his haste to answer it, Lee tripped over a chair, fell against the table, and jostled the phone to the floor. He attempted to catch it but it slipped through his fingers. By the time he retrieved and answered it, Tao, Sophie, and Monica had collapsed on the couch in laughter.

His face bright red, Lee glared at them as he listened to his mother's voice.

"Goodness," she said, "what was that?"

"Nothing," he said. "I dropped the phone."

"Oh," she said, "well, your Ba ba wishes to see you and Tao this afternoon. Something about a charter."

"Sure," he said. "What time?"

"Two," she said. "Bring my daughters. I have things for them."

"Okay," he said.

With exaggerated care, he placed the phone on the table.

"Shut up you three!"

Giggling, Sophie hugged him. He squeezed her as she kissed him.

"Are you okay?" she asked.

"Other than a slightly dented dignity," he said.

Tao was wiping tears from his face. It was good to hear him laugh. To Lee that was worth the humiliation.

"Ba ba wants to see us at 2:00 about a charter," he said. "And Mama wants the two of you for something."

They took time to eat lunch, then drove to Kai Chi and Meng's.

Meng immediately swept the girls away with her to let the men talk business. Lee wondered what she was up to as he watched her whispering conspiratorially to them.

Kai Chi ushered him and Tao into his office.

It amazed Lee how untraditional his parents' house was; thoroughly Western in design and set up. Save for the gardens, private quarters, and some of the décor, there was very little Chinese about it. In a way it bothered him. His father had strayed far from his own culture.

He and Tao took a seat in the comfortable leather chairs in front of Kai Chi's desk as he leaned against the edge of it.

"Your Uncle Kim wishes to charter the yacht for an outing with some of his colleagues day after tomorrow. He asked me to arrange it and see you were paid in advance."

"Why didn't he set it up himself?" Lee asked.

Kai Chi glanced at his nephew.

"I am afraid," he said, "he finds it difficult to deal with Tao, especially after what happened at Meng's birthday."

"That fiasco was Taibo's doing," he said. "He's the one Kim should have difficulty dealing with. What's Tao ever done to him? What's his problem?"

"I think," Kai Chi said, "it's more to do with Kong than Tao. Kim was angry when Kong defied him. He sees only Kong when he looks at Tao. I think the memory is difficult for him."

"I'm not my father," Tao said.

He got to his feet. He had no idea why his parents left Hong Kong. If there was a rift between Kong and Kim, it had nothing to do with him.

"I don't even remember him," he said.

Kai Chi and Lee stared at him. He sank into the chair. It was true. After so much of his childhood was spent in and out of foster homes, the memory of his parents became confused until he wasn't sure if he remembered them or if they were jumbled together with the others.

"You don't remember?"

For Kai Chi it was a terrible revelation. It meant the years Tao had spent alone, he hadn't even his parents' memories to sustain him.

Tao took a deep breath and shook his head.

"Most of what happened before the day they were killed is a blank," he said. "The doctors said I shut everything away to protect myself. Maybe I did. All I remember before then is Lee. Nothing else."

He looked to his cousin.

"After the accident when I was six, I clung to Lee. I guess I kept clinging to him like an anchor. Don't ask me why. Mama and Ba ba were gone. I don't remember…"

He left it hanging. Lee stole a glance at his father.

"I don't care what Kim sees when he looks at me," Tao said. "If he wants the charter, that's why we're in business. If he's too much of a coward to face me, then he can deal with Lee. I'd rather he did."

Kai Chi noticed Tao hadn't said Uncle Kim. He couldn't blame him for that.

"Tell Uncle Kim," Lee said, "to have his party at the slip at noon day after tomorrow. We leave at 1:00. Anyone not there by that time gets left behind. That includes him."

He stood.

"Tell him to leave the money with you. Oh, and tell him to leave Taibo at home. I don't want anymore trouble on our yacht.

Kai Chi nodded.

"You may also inform Uncle," Lee said, "that if he ever wants another charter, he comes directly to us. If not, the answer will be no."

"I'll see to the arrangements," Kai Chi said.

He wouldn't argue. He wouldn't dare argue. He was proud of the stand Lee took. He understood, even if Tao didn't, why it was Lee Tao held onto over the years. In the winds of adversity, it was the steadfast ones who stood. Those who bent were in danger of being crushed under the weight, as he had been in the past. He decided that would be no more. Kim might be the oldest, but his decisions and directions were wrong. It was time for a change.

"Shall we find our wives?" he asked. "Speaking of which, when are you and Sophie getting married?"

"I don't know," Lee said.

"Well, don't you think you should?" Kai Chi asked. "You live together, sleep together no doubt. If you're to be man and wife, you should be man and wife."

Tao ducked his head and turned to intently study the painting hanging on the wall.

"Ba ba," Lee said, clearing his throat, "you're talking to the wrong person. I asked. She hasn't—I mean she said she'd come to Hong Kong with me, but…"

Kai Chi grasped him firmly by the arm and steered him out of the office and towards the interior of the house.

"Then we shall ask again," he said.

Tao muffled a snort of laughter.

Meng was showing the girls some old photo albums in the atrium and they glanced up as the men entered. Kai Chi herded Lee to stand directly in front of Sophie before he released him and stepped away.

Lee squirmed. Sophie looked at him questioningly.

"We've been in Hong Kong for three months now," he said. "Before we left the States, I asked you a question. I want to ask you again."

He glanced at his father, who nodded encouragement. Lee took Sophie's hand and sank to one knee.

"Sophie, will—will you marry me?" he asked.

He held his breath. He was nervous and thought that was strange. But what if she did say no? He didn't know what he'd do if she didn't agree.

"Yes," she said.

He wasn't sure he'd heard her right.

"What?"

She laughed and caressed his face with her hand.

"Yes, silly. I said yes before."

He began to breathe again and clumsily got to his feet.

"When?" Kai Chi asked.

Meng dug a sharp elbow into his ribs.

"When Lee's ready," Sophie said.

"I'm ready now," Lee said.

His face turned red.

"I mean I was ready the first time I asked."

"We'll have a proper wedding," Kai Chi said. "You must make plans. What day? What time? Who do you want to invite? I must contact your brothers."

"Ba ba!" Lee said.

"Kai Chi!" Meng chided. "Leave the children alone. Now you caused enough embarrassment."

She pushed him to the other side of the table and into a chair.

"Sit, all of you," Meng said. "I'll fix tea and we'll celebrate."

She looked to Sophie and winked. Sophie winked back. Monica giggled. Tao and Lee wondered if something more had been going on than they were aware. Maybe it hadn't been just Kai Chi who was doing all the planning.

Chapter 13

When Lee looked at the clock, it was almost 3:00 in the morning. He took a deep breath. His mouth felt like cotton and his head ached.

After the celebratory tea, Kai Chi had brought out a bottle of his best wine to toast the coming nuptials, then a second bottle to toast the couple, and a third just to toast in general.

Because of his medication, Tao was the only one not drinking. He was the only one sober by the time they poured into the car and headed home. Monica was asleep when they pulled up in front of the apartment. Tao carried her to their room then returned to the car to retrieve Sophie who complained of having trouble finding her feet. He carried her to her room and went for Lee.

Lee somehow managed to climb the stairs without assistance, though he wasn't exactly sure how. He did require Tao's shoulder to get him to the bedroom where he fell into bed next to Sophie.

Tao pulled Lee's shoes, socks, and shirt off before tucking the blankets around him, but left Sophie as she was, shoes and all. He made sure the blanket covered her.

One of her heels dug into the calf of Lee's right leg. He carefully moved it aside and removed her shoes from her feet before he eased out of bed and stumbled into the bathroom. Relieved, he went into the livingroom and found Tao by the window looking into the night. Tao glanced at him as he dropped into a chair.

"What are you doing up?" Lee asked.

Tao shrugged and turned back to his vigil at the window. Lee watched him. He thought he understood what was bothering him.

"Don't let what Uncle Kim thinks get to you," he said.

"I don't care what he thinks," Tao said.

"Then what's bothering you?" Lee asked.

Tao sighed and turned, jamming his hands into his jeans' pockets.

"I don't like the idea of this charter," he said.

Lee knew Tao's premonitions were worth heeding. If he thought something was wrong, Lee wanted to know what.

"Wanna tell me why?" he asked.

Tao paced.

"There's something not right about it," he said. "Something more than just Kim's dislike for me."

Lee sat forward, elbows resting on his knees.

"Like what?"

"I don't know," he said. "I can't explain it. It's just a feeling I have. I don't like it. When you're a cop, you learn fast to instinctively read people. If you don't, you die."

He paused.

"It's a gut feeling. There's wrongness to Kim. I felt it from the first. I know this feeling. I've had it hundreds of times over hundreds of people"

Lee wasn't sure what about Kim Tao meant, but he trusted his instincts, as well as he trusted his own. He didn't like Kim and he didn't trust him either.

"I don't like him chartering the yacht," Tao said. "It feels like trouble."

"Should we cancel then?" Lee asked.

Tao shook his head.

"No, I won't give him the satisfaction. Maybe that's what he wants. I want to know what he's up to. We need to keep our eyes and ears open. We could get caught in a crossfire."

It made Lee uneasy that Tao was so worried. He had an almost psychic connection to situations and circumstances. Lee remembered Bryson's words.

Work is all he does, all he thinks, all he lives.

All the next day as he and Tao cleaned and readied the yacht, he thought about it. Twice he saw Taibo lurking on the pier. One look at Tao told him he'd seen him too. Tao saw everything. His body was tense, every nerve aware of the environment around him, every smell, every movement, what belonged and what didn't.

Tiger, Lee thought inwardly.

Meng arranged to meet the girls early. She had a special destination in mind and led them to a prominent bridal shop in the heart of Hong Kong.

Sophie and Monica wandered among every conceivable style of wedding dress. The purely traditional Chinese wedding attire to the most modern of Western and European style dresses all bore designer labels and the price tags to go with them. Each time they looked at a price tag, they gasped. The gowns were far too extravagant for Sophie and Lee's finances.

One gown, Sophie fell instantly in love with it, but knew there was no way she could afford it. Meng watched her. She went to Sophie's side and looked at the price.

"Is this the one?" she asked.

Sophie smiled and ran her hand wistfully over the satin of the gown.

"I wish," she said. "It's so beautiful. But there's no way Lee or I could afford this."

Meng looked at the size. The gown was too large. She signaled one of the sales assistants.

"Does this come in a smaller size?"

The assistant nodded.

"What size?" Meng asked Sophie.

"Oh no, Meng," Sophie said. "Not this. Really. It's much too expensive."

Meng straightened to her full height, which brought her to Sophie's shoulders, and gave her daughter-to-be a stern look.

"I will decide what is and is not too expensive," she said. "My sons all married in Australia. I was unable to do this for my other daughters-in-law. This is my wedding gift for you."

"You'll look angelic in that," Monica said.

Sophie didn't argue. She did want the dress. She didn't know what to say.

"*Dohje*," she said. "Thank you, Meng. You're wonderful."

She threw her arms around her future mother-in-law and hugged her.

They saw to the fitting and chose a petticoat and veil. Sophie picked out her garters and a gown for Monica who would be her Matron-of-Honor.

Next, Meng took them to a florist to choose flowers for the bouquets. They decided the wedding would be held in the house gardens with the bride and groom saying their vows on the little bridge spanning the brook. It would be a fairytale setting. They couldn't wait to tell Lee and Tao.

Chapter 14

By the time Tao and Lee returned, Sophie and Monica were in bed. Two plates of cold food sat on the dining table along with a note.

Thanks for letting us know you'd be home late. Enjoy your dinner!

Lee read the note and sank glumly into a chair. He passed the note to Tao.

"I think we're in trouble," he said, rubbing his aching forehead.

Tao dropped into a chair and ran his hand over his face. He looked at the plates of congealing food and grimaced.

It'd been a long day. They'd worked hard preparing the yacht for the next day's tour. Lee knew something was eating at Tao that he wasn't talking about and they'd spent the day snapping at each. They were tired, disgruntled, and now depressed.

Tao stared at his plate. The sight of food made him ill. With an angry scowl, he shoved the plate away.

"I'm going to bed," he said. "That is if she'll let me in."

Lee carried the plates to the kitchen and dumped their contents into the trash. He would wash the dishes later. He didn't like wasting food, but at this point in time he didn't care.

Tao went to the bedroom and quietly undressed. He wanted to shower, but was too tired. He slipped between the sheets aware of Monica's back to him. He knew she was awake. He felt her tension.

"Are you mad at me?" he asked.

He felt her stiffen.

"Right now, yes."

"Really?"

She heard the desperate catch in his voice and propped herself on her elbow to face him. His eyes held that lost little boy expression and she softened, but didn't let him see it. She was angry and wanted him to understand why.

"You hurt my feelings," she said. "Lee hurt Sophie's. We had something we wanted to celebrate with you and you two didn't have the decency to pick up the phone."

"I know," he said. "I'm really sorry."

He was too capitulating. She didn't quite think he understood.

"It may not seem like much," she said. "But Sophie gave up a lot to come to Hong Kong with Lee. She gave up her nursing career and left her home because she loves him. It's not easy for her to play the housewife, because she used to having that career. He can't just take that for granted."

"What about what you gave up?" Tao asked.

"What did I give up? Being a waitress? I'm used to waiting on people."

"I'm serious, Nikki," he said.

"I know," she said. "I left because I love you. But I didn't leave that much behind."

"You're right," he said. "about us being inconsiderate. We've been taking both of you for granted. I guess we don't think about what you do all day."

"What happened?" she asked. "Something's bothering you."

"Bad day," he said. "Lee and I were at each others throats all day long. I don't know what's wrong. Just—a bad day."

That caught her off guard. She'd never seen them at odds, had never given much thought about the possibility.

"What did you want to celebrate?" Tao asked.

"We'll discuss it tomorrow," she said. "Right now, I think we need to go to sleep."

The moonlight caught the glint of a tear in the corner of Tao's eye. She was the only person to ever see his tears and then only when he was too worn out to hold them back.

"I accept your apology," she said, "but we will have a long talk tomorrow, and not just about tonight."

She kissed his mouth. His arms slid around her and pulled her to his chest. She lay her cheek against it and listened to the strong, steady beating of his heart. She remembered the night she'd met him, how much she'd wanted to love him, to make love to him, even without knowing anything about him. Now she did know and wanted him more than ever.

She kissed his skin and massaged his hard stomach with the palm of her hand. He pulled her tighter to him and breathed in the scent of her hair. She considered how easily his tears came their first night together. It was the pain of ages eking from him and she'd been glad of it. Someday, that pain would all be gone and he would be able to smile and laugh easily. Until then, and even after, she would love him as much as that first night.

"I love you," he whispered as her touched feathered over him.

Lee slipped into bed hoping not to wake Sophie. She wasn't asleep.

"I want to talk to you," she said. "Tomorrow, mister, we will talk."

He gritted his teeth against the guilt he felt. She meant it.

"Yes, dear."

"Don't make fun of me. Where were you?"

"I'm not making fun of you," he said. "I promise, I'm not. And we were on the yacht. We had a bad day, both of us. Tao and I were at each other's throats all day long. That's no excuse. I should have called. I just had a lot on my mind and didn't think. Forgive me?"

She studied him with a pout on her lips.

"Don't ever do that again," she said.

"I won't. I promise," he said.

She wasn't really angry. That surprised him. She had every right to be. He had been taking her for granted, too concerned with everything else.

"I am sorry," he said, this time seriously meaning it.

She kissed him again as she snuggled close to his side. Her fingers traced across his chest. He squirmed.

"Just be glad I love you, you big dummy," she said.

Trying to escape the tickling fingers, he pulled her into a deep kiss.

"You don't know how much I am," he said.

"Oh," she said, pulling away. "I forgot. Kai Chi called. He said he needed to talk to you as soon as you came home."

Lee glanced at the clock. It was after midnight. He removed her hand from his chest and kissed her fingers. Kai Chi would have to wait a bit longer. He pulled Sophie back into his embrace and kiss. He had more important things to do first.

71

Chapter 15

The phone woke Lee. His voice was thick with sleep when he answered.

"You didn't call," Kai Chi said.

Carefully, Lee moved his arm from under Sophie's neck and rolled onto his side.

"Ba ba," he said, "it's 4:00 in the morning!"

He ran his hand through his hair and wished he had a drink of water. His mouth felt dry and tasted sour.

"I know what time it is," Kai Chi said. "I waited all night."

"Well what's so important that it won't wait?" Lee asked.

"The charter for tomorrow is canceled," Kai Chi said.

"*Mat ye a*!" Lee sat up.

Sophie stirred and mumbled something. He glanced at her and lowered his voice.

"What?"

"Kim," Kai Chi said. "said he decided to wait so you can concentrate on the wedding. He contacted his business associates and changed the date."

"Why didn't he contact us?" Lee asked.

"Calm down, *jai*," his father said. "Be thankful. Now you've nothing to distract you."

There was no way Lee believed Kim was acting out of consideration. There had to be an alternate reason. It didn't matter. It made him angry that his Uncle hadn't the courtesy to contact him directly.

"There's nothing to interrupt your preparations," Kai Chi said. "We only have a week. I've ordered the decorations to be delivered tomorrow. The food is catered. The wedding cake is ordered. All that's left is for you and Tao to get tuxedoes."

"Did you leave anything for Sophie and me to do?" Lee asked.

Kai Chi ignored his sarcasm.

"You have friends you want to come?" he asked. "Make a list. I'll see they get here."

Lee closed his eyes and counted to 10.

"Ba ba, you're pushing," he said.

There was a pause.

"I know," Kai Chi said. "I'm just pleased for you. Sophie is already like a daughter to me."

He paused again.

"I'm also proud of you, *jai*. I don't want you to worry. I want you and Sophie to concentrate only on each other."

Lee leaned against his propped pillows and sighed.

"You're going overboard," he said. "I do appreciate the thought, Ba ba. You know Tao will be furious. We fought all day long. It was all we seemed to be able to do."

"Fought?" Kai Chi asked. "About what?"

"Nothing," Lee said, "and everything. My legs hurt. His back and head hurt. He was mad about the way the charter was arranged. I was irritated because he was in such a lousy humor. We managed to top off the evening by making the girls mad when we didn't make it home for dinner."

"Didn't you call?" Kai Chi asked.

"No."

"Never keep a lady waiting," Kai Chi said. "Especially if she is or soon will be your wife. Your Mama taught me that long ago. Is that why you delayed calling me?"

Lee growled under his breath.

"I'm not saying. Is that all you had to tell me?"

"Yes." Kai Chi laughed. "I didn't want you to show up and have nothing but an empty boat tomorrow—today."

"Thanks for that anyway," Lee said.

"Go back to sleep," Kai Chi said. "See you later."

Lee put the phone on the holder and frowned at the far wall. The cancellation, especially after the trouble the charter had caused in the first place, was a bad omen. He didn't believe the postponement was out of the goodness of Kim's heart. There had to be another reason otherwise.

He scooted down into the covers. Sophie cuddled close and draped her arm across his chest. He felt her warm lips kiss his chest. He closed his eyes to hold the feelings rippling through him.

The phone jangling made him jump. Sophie came fully awake and sat up as startled as he was. She glared at the offending phone, climbed out of bed, and went into the bathroom.

Lee snatched the phone from its base.

"Yes?"

"Hey, pal, is that any way to greet a friend?"

The voice on the other end was cheerful and familiar.

"Hey, Patrick," Lee said, "nice surprise to hear your voice. What's up?"

"Ah, y'know," Patrick said, "not much. Same old stuff—except now I'm Captain of this outfit."

He paused for effect and wasn't disappointed.

"That's fantastic!" Lee said. "Patrick, I'm proud of ya, pal."

"Thanks," Patrick said. "I figured you'd never forgive me if I didn't tell you. So how're things in Hong Kong? You doin' okay?"

Lee settled into his pillows. Patrick Swayne was his oldest and dearest friend in America. They had served together on the New York Fire Department and Patrick followed him when he made Captain of their station in Chinatown. He had also been a great help with Tao after the shooting.

"I would've called you soon," Lee said. "Sophie and I are getting married at the end of the week. You do want to come, right?"

There was a whistle that nearly ruptured his eardrum. He held the phone away for a second.

"Oh, sorry," Patrick said. "It's just I'm happy for ya. And you know I'd love to come, but…"

"But nothing," Lee said. "Ba ba's offered to pay the airfare. If I didn't want you here so badly, I wouldn't let him. Right now, it's the only way to get you here."

"What about Tao?" Patrick asked. "You know how he feels about me."

"I'm not marrying Tao," he said. "As long as you don't try and stuff him into the back of an ambulance, he'll be fine."

They both laughed. Patrick agreed to come and to ask anyone else interested in getting a free trip to Hong Kong. He said he would let Lee know the final count. They said good-bye just as Sophie returned from the bathroom, a pout on her face. Her hair was sleep wild and the light that streamed through the window backlit her lacy white short nightgown so every curve underneath showed.

"Come here," Lee said.

She went to him and took his hand.

"Who was that?" she asked.

"Patrick," he said as he leaned forward to kiss her.

Her arms slid around his neck. He felt the heat from her and knew she wanted him as much as he wanted her.

"He's coming to the wedding," he whispered.

The phone rang.

"Let Tao get it," Sophie whispered, her lips pressed hungrily against his.

The phone continued to ring.

"If you answer that damn phone," Sophie said, "I'll bite you."

Lee let the phone ring as their bodies melded into one, their minds shut to all but the two of them—and the stupid insistent phone that refused to stop ringing. Whoever it was wasn't giving up. Unfortunately, they had turned the answering machine off. Unable to stand the distraction, Lee jerked the phone off of its base.

"Wei!" he said, partly in irritation, partly from the bite Sophie inflicted on his chest.

"I must speak to Wong Tai Chi."

The voice was soft, Chinese, formal, and female.

Chapter 16

Lee heard a click on the extension and knew Tao had finally picked it up.

Sophie was insistent. She wanted him off the phone and paying attention to her.

"Call back tomorrow," he said and started to hang up.

He knew Tao was listening.

"I must speak to Tao," the woman insisted.

Lee'd had enough. Sophie wouldn't wait.

"Dammit, Tao, answer the phone!" he yelled, and dropped the receiver to set his mind on more important things.

"What do you want, Ling?" Tao asked.

He'd recognized her voice even after so many years. He didn't want to talk to her, couldn't imagine how she'd gotten his phone number. He would've been happy if Lee had just hung up. By the strain in Lee's voice, he had a good idea what he and Sophie were doing.

He glanced at Monica who was propped on her elbow to listen. They, too, had been occupied when the phone rang. It'd taken him a moment to reach the phone. By that time, Lee had answered.

Monica's hand rested on his arm to let him know she was there for his support.

"You know who?"

Ling sounded surprised.

"I know your voice," he said. "Remember? What do you want?"

"I must see you," she said. "Today, noon, at the Chung How Restaurant."

"No," he said.

"This is not a request," she said. "You will come. It's important to you."

He sat up, his hand tightening on the receiver as if to strangle her by way of it.

76

"I'm not your servant. Why should you want to see a ghost? I hear that's what I am to you."

Ling spoke with an icy edge.

"You will come," she said. "You will talk. You have a son."

"Mat ye a? Nei hai mat ye yi si ah?"

He glanced at Monica again and repeated in English.

"What do you mean?" he asked Ling.

"I think it's clear enough," she said.

He shook his head in disbelief as anger ripped through him. Monica tightened her grip on his arm.

"Ni go hai gong daai wa!" he said. "You're lying! *Nie hai mat ye a?"*

Monica shook his arm. He shrugged away from her.

"I told you," Ling said. "Be at the restaurant today, noon. If you are not, I tell your Uncle this secret."

"Uncle Kai Chi won't believe you," he said, "and he won't care."

He was shaking with rage. It wasn't true, couldn't be. There was no possible way. Ling and he had shared only one night together. Even on their wedding night, she'd refused to let him near her. Life wouldn't be that cruel, not after all he'd been through.

"But your Uncle Kim will," Ling said and slammed down the phone.

"Ling! Ling!"

With a roar he dropped the receiver in the cradle of the phone. He felt dizzy and sick.

"What Tao?" Monica touched his arm again.

This time he didn't flinch.

Ten years! For 10 years he had lived with Ling's silence. If there had been a child, her family would have wasted no time making him pay. She wanted something. He was certain of it, but what? Revenge? Money? He knew she was lying. She had to be lying.

He felt sick and leaned his forehead against the blankets.

But what if it was true? It wasn't impossible.

Monica pulled him to her and held tight. She had no idea what Ling had said, but she was determined to find out and make Ling regret it.

"It's okay," she whispered, caressing his hair as she rocked him in her arms. "It's okay."

His anger and grief radiated through his skin into hers.

Lee and Sophie appeared at the bedroom door. They'd heard Tao's bellow. Lee had rushed into his jeans and into their room with Sophie wrapped in her robe on his heels.

"Mat ye si a?" he asked. "What's the matter? What happened?"

Tao shook his head, unable to answer. He shrugged their arms away, scrambled out of bed, and ran to the bathroom where they heard him throw up. Monica grabbed his robe and went to him. She led him back to the bed and he sat down, his face pale and hot.

"What did she say?" Lee asked. "What's she up to? What did she tell you?"

Tao took several deep breaths and managed to repeat the phone conversation.

"It's not true," Lee said.

"Of course it's not true," Sophie said.

"It could be," Tao said.

"But it's not," Monica said. "How can it be?"

He stared at her. He hadn't realized until that moment how angry she was and the glint in her blue eyes was one he hadn't seen before.

She looked straight at him.

"She slept with you," she said. "She probably slept with others before and after you. If she has a child, it could belong to anyone."

Tao shook his head, not sure one-way or the other.

"We're assuming there is a child," Lee said. "What if there isn't? I think she's up to something."

"But why?" Tao asked.

"Money," Sophie said. "Why else?"

"Why now?" Tao countered. "Why wait for 10 years and then come up with this now?"

"Because she didn't know you were in Hong Kong until she saw you at Kai Chi's party," Sophie said.

"It doesn't make sense," Lee said. "Tao's right. If she wanted money, why now? Her husband makes a good living from what I heard."

"Maybe she doesn't get any of his money," Sophie said. "Or maybe he's in trouble and needs money."

"He works for his father," Lee said.

"Maybe his father doesn't pay him much," Monica said. "Maybe he needs money and he can't ask his father because he's wimp. He'd have to be a wimp to marry her."

"I was married to her," Tao said.

She kissed him.

"That doesn't count. You barely knew her and you aren't married to her now," she said. "You didn't stay with her and let daddy run your life. You're not a wimp."

"We're getting off the subject," Sophie said.

"Which is?" Lee asked.

"If she's bluffing," Sophie said.

"There's only one way to find out," Monica said.

She touched Tao's cheek.

"And we'll do it together."

Chapter 17

Tao wasn't alone when he arrived at the restaurant. Lee, Monica, and Sophie followed close behind him as he approached the table where Ling sat. It was obvious, she hadn't expected him to be accompanied.

Once Tao thought Ling to be the most beautiful girl he'd ever seen. That memory of why he had loved her made him cold. All he felt for her now was contempt.

Ling said nothing, just handed him a picture of a small boy. Chinese children tended to look younger than they were, but to Tao's trained policeman's eyes the picture of the boy with a head full of blue-black hair and deep brown eyes held nothing of himself and nothing of Ling either.

"What do you want, Ling?" he asked as he returned the photo to her.

His question was put straightforward, without rancor. Ling squirmed nervously under his gaze.

"I told you," she said in Cantonese.

"*Ying man!*" he said. "English!"

His forcefulness made her jump.

"This is wrong, Ling," he said. "Why wait until now? You had all those years to tell me. Why are you doing this?"

She sat in a defiant posture, her hands in her lap, her eyes fixed on his face.

Monica noticed the long fingers twining around and around. The nervous fidgeting had to mean Ling was lying. There had been that remote possibility, but the moment Monica looked at the photo, she knew the child wasn't his.

"I told him," Ling said, "that his father died before he was born. I couldn't tell him you abandoned us. I didn't think you would ever return to Hong Kong. When I saw you at Wong Kai Chi's party, I felt it only right that he and you knew the truth."

Lee reached for the photo and studied the round face, the slanted eyes, every feature of the boy.

"Why are you doing this?" he asked. "What is it you want? Do you need money? Is that what this is all about?"

Her eyes snapped around to him. She straightened rigidly. Lee thought she looked frightened.

"My husband knows the truth," she said. "I have been married only a short while. I couldn't hide a 10 year old son from him."

She returned her attention to Tao.

"Your son. You're responsible for him."

Monica saw all the signs of a desperate woman.

"It is money," she said. "You need money."

Sophie had come to the same conclusion. Women's intuition—something the men would never understand, but they knew. So did Ling. She was angered by their intrusion, but they didn't care.

"I want my son's birthright," Ling said. "I want his father to do the honorable thing."

Monica came abruptly to her feet and hovered over her.

"You stay away from my husband, you little bitch!" she said.

"Monica!" Tao was startled by her outburst.

"And take your stupid little games someplace else or I swear . . ." she continued.

Ling also came to her feet and moved out of Monica's reach.

Tao grabbed Monica, afraid she might do something she shouldn't.

Lee was behind them ready to grab Tao if he turned on Ling. He wasn't sure which of the three he should watch.

The situation was getting out of hand and the rest of the people in the restaurant were watching nervously as the waiters prepared to step in.

"I would suggest," Sophie said, "if you want the father to do the honorable thing then you should go and find him."

She looked directly into Ling's face.

"Tao is not the father of this child." She shoved the picture at Ling. "You know it. How dare you treat your own child, if it is yours, as a pawn. Your husband is rich. Surely if you need money, he can give it to you."

"If it's money you need," Tao said, still holding a struggling Monica, "you won't get it from me—ever. You told me you wanted nothing to do with me. Now I'm telling you."

"I will tell Kim," she threatened.

"Tell him whatever you want," Tao said. "I can take care of this once and for all. Produce the kid. I'll have a DNA test done. We'll see who's telling the truth."

She held his gaze, but only for a moment. Fear was written on her face. He saw it. It made him pause. Something wasn't right.

"Whose child is it that you're so afraid?" he asked in a softer tone.

She wavered. He thought she might give in and tell him. Instead she marched out of the restaurant without answering.

Tao sank into a chair. Lee sat next to him and placed a hand on his shoulder. The girls sat down as an apprehensive waiter appeared at the table. All of the guests in the restaurant seemed to breathe a sigh of relief. It was one of the reasons Tao insisted they speak English.

"Do you wish to order?" the waiter asked.

Lee started to shake his head, but Tao nodded. He needed time to calm down.

Lee picked up the menu and ordered for all of them. He knew it didn't matter what. He also ordered drinks. They all needed something strong after what they'd just gone through.

The drinks arrived and then their meal. They ate in silence. Monica noticed Tao only picked at what was on his plate. She wished he would eat something.

"What do you think she'll do?" she asked.

"She won't have the test done," Tao said. "She knows she can't prove it. If her motive is money, she won't spend anymore trying to convince us."

"Why did she do this?" Sophie asked. "What could she possibly gain by it? She really didn't believe you'd fall for it, did she?"

Tao offered a lopsided grin. Had he been alone, he wasn't so sure he wouldn't have.

"What I wonder," Lee said as he studied his wine glass, "is why she threatened to tell Uncle Kim. What possible motive was that?"

Tao said nothing. He was asking himself the same question. He didn't like the fact Kim's name had surfaced. That was strange. He wondered what connection Ling had to Kim.

"I think after dinner we should go find our tuxedos," he said. "We don't have much time and I need something normal after this bit of insanity."

Chapter 18

Tao was quiet at dinner that night. He said very little after they left the restaurant. He let Monica and Sophie choose the tuxedos and was fitted without comment. They walked about the city most of the day trying to get the incident with Ling out of their minds.

All the walking made his back and head ache. He felt sick to his stomach and wanted to find a place away from everyone.

Lee's legs had started hurting and he suggested they decline the dinner invitation when Kai Chi called after they returned to the apartment. Tao thought they should go, even though he wasn't hungry.

The girls didn't think it was a good idea because they could see how much the men were hurting. Tao argued it wouldn't be right to refuse the invitation considering how much Kai Chi had done for them. The truth was he hoped to question his uncle about Kim.

Lee watched him now across the dinner table. He saw the tired worry lines at the corner of Tao's eyes and mouth. Tao's life seemed to constantly be filled with turmoil. And Tao wasn't eating, which was always a bad sign. He hadn't eaten much in the past few days. He would have to speak to him about it.

Meng watched her son and her nephew. From the moment they had arrived, she'd seen the crisis on both of their faces and wondered what had happened. Before the meal, she'd hoped one or the other would tell, but so far neither one had said anything.

She glanced at Kai Chi and saw he, too, was watching and waiting, but it was the girls who did all the talking. They went on about shopping for the tuxedos and how they'd found a few more things for the apartment, but they talked too fast and too much. It wasn't like them.

Meng was about to lose her patience. She had about as much as she could stand. She opened her mouth to demand that someone talk when a crash and a bellow from the front of the house brought them all to their feet.

A second later, Kim stormed into the dining room followed by two other men.

Lee recognized the men immediately. He had seen them the night of the party. The older was Ling's father-in-law. The younger man, Lee assumed, was Ling's husband.

Kim's face was scarlet with rage as he pointed his finger in Tao's direction.

"You," he said. "You dishonor this family."

Tao held his ground, his gaze steady, his fists balled at his sides. He clenched his jaws with forced restraint.

"Kim!" Kai Chi said. "How dare you storm my home like this. Have you forgotten how to knock?"

"I dare," Kim said, "when this worthless whelp brings dishonor onto this house and our family."

Monica moved protectively to Tao's side. She wasn't sure if Tao made a move towards Kim if she would try to stop him or let him go and join him. She couldn't understand what they were saying. They were speaking Cantonese too rapidly for her to understand, but she didn't have to know the words. Their body language was enough.

"First he brings dishonor by abandoning his family and wife for America," Kim said, "Now he dishonors her and us again by denying the child that is his through his union before marriage with Lei Ling."

"What?" Kai Chi asked. He looked to Tao then to Lee.

Meng moved to the other side of Tao and placed a protective arm around him.

Tao couldn't help his reaction. It was so ludicrous he burst into a frightening laugh edged with anguish and fury.

"Abandoned?"

The laughter vanished. Raw hatred flared and his tone was razor sharp.

"I didn't abandon her or anyone else," he said.

He looked directly at Kim.

"If I remember right," he said, "she didn't want me and you threw me out."

Lee's head snapped around to stare at his Uncle. Kai Chi pressed his lips together and watched his son. Lee had never known the truth about that.

"Ling is lying," Tao said. "And if anyone is bringing dishonor it's you. Why do you care? It's none of your business. Back off and leave me alone."

Kim said nothing, just glared at his nephew. The older man with him made a lunge towards Tao. Tao turned ready to fight. Meng grabbed his arm. The man stopped.

Lee had noticed Ling's husband hadn't moved. During the confrontation, he stood silently to one side. Lee saw no malice, only what looked to him like embarrassment.

Tao fought to control a calm he didn't possess. Meng had a firm grip on one of his arms. Monica held tight to the other. If he struggled, they'd have let him go. He'd thought it all behind him, all the hurt, all the anger, but it lingered, seethed, like a demon.

"Kim," Kai Chi said, "what is this all about? What child?"

Before Kim could answer, Lee told him about the phone call the night before, about the confrontation in the restaurant, and about Tao's solution as to prove paternity.

"Did Ling take the child to be tested as Tao suggested?" Kai Chi asked.

He was doing his best to keep things from escalating out of control, although he was tempted to start something. Kim might be the head of the Wong family, but he had no right to invade their home and throw unsubstantiated accusations at one of Kai Chi's family.

"My son's wife is under no obligation to do any such thing," Ling's father-in-law said.

"If she wished to prove Tao was the father, she must," Meng said. "Otherwise her allegations mean nothing."

"You have been against Tao from the moment he returned to Hong Kong," Kai Chi said. "I don't understand why, but I won't have it. He is my son now, and I won't have you offend him without offending me. Now get out of my house and take these men with you. When you have proof this preposterous claim in true, then we'll talk."

"You'll regret your refusal to do the honorable thing," Kim said to Tao. "I'll see to it."

"You'd better stay out of my way," Tao warned.

Kim turned on his heel and went out. Ling's father-in-law followed, but her husband remained and took a step towards Tao. Tao thought he saw resignation on the man's face as he glanced over his shoulder to make certain his father and Kim were gone.

"Ling was put up to this," her husband said. "Know that. The child isn't yours. It isn't hers. I'm sorry."

He dropped his gaze and bowed slightly before leaving.

Lee whirled on his father.

"What's going on? What's this all about? What's Kim got to do with Ling and her family?"

He took a step towards his father.

"And what did Tao mean when he said Kim threw him out?"

Kai Chi shook his head. He had no answers for his son. Kim was playing Tao, but he had no idea to what end. Kai Chi did know his brother was close to detonating a bomb. If his persecution continued, not only would Tao explode, but Lee as well.

"Well?" Lee asked.

"I can't tell you," Kai Chi said. "I don't know the answers. And about the other matter—not now."

The dinner was over. Their food had grown cold and no one had any appetite left.

Monica wanted to take Tao home. She was proud of him for not losing his temper, but it had been too close. She had felt his trembling through the palms of her hands.

As they said goodnight, Lee told his father, "I want answers, Ba ba."

Kai Chi said nothing as Meng kissed Lee on the cheek and whispered something to him. Whatever it was didn't calm him down, but he nodded. She kissed Monica on the cheek and told her to take Tao home and love him. She smiled encouragement at all four of them as they went out the door. When they were gone, she turned on Kai Chi. She wanted some explanations.

Tao was experiencing feelings he didn't like. Questions whirled in his head. In bed, he lay awake long after everyone else was asleep. He stared at the ceiling and went over what had happened at dinner.

Monica stirred at his side, her soft breathing a salve to his jangled nerves. Something niggled in the back of his mind. It had something to do with Kim and it gnawed at him. It was hours before he finally went to sleep.

He looked into his father's face. Kong smiled at him as they lifted the crates in the storage area of the new market. They heard the tinkle of the bell over the door then a deep demanding voice. Tao didn't understand the words. They were in English. Kong's eyes narrowed in alarm as he ran towards the front of the market. Tao started to follow, but Kong ordered him to stay where he was.

There was an angry shout and a scream just as Kong reached the entrance from the back room to the store. There was a pop followed by another and Kong fell back through the door, landing on his back at Tao's feet. The voices laughed and Tao heard his mother scream again.

He stood in the door, transfixed by the scene in front of him. Men he didn't know took money from the register, food, beer, and other items from the shelves. One man held Tia to the floor, her dress hiked over her bare thighs. The man grunted and moved, his huge hand held over her mouth as she fought him and struggled to scream. Her eyes found her son's.

She managed to free an arm from under the man's knee. She struck him hard across the cheek, her nails bringing blood. For a second her mouth was free as he drew his hand back.

"Tao, faai jau!"

The man pulled a gun from his belt and shot her in the face before turning toward the door. Tao ran and slid into the freezer where he hid behind the hanging meats. He made himself as small as possible and listened to the sound of his racing heart and ragged sobs. He was cold and terrified. He heard footsteps coming. The handle of the door turned. It opened. Someone stood silhouetted in the light.

"Mama!"

His eyes opened to the ceiling above him. It was dark. The air was cold. Sweat rolled off of him. He shook, the memory of the nightmare vivid in his mind. He took deep breaths to calm his pounding heart. He glanced over at Monica and was relived that she was still asleep. His scream had only been in his mind.

There was a hammer inside of his head. His back protested as he eased to his feet and went to the kitchen to fix some tea. The sun was at the base of the horizon, a collage of purple, orange, red, and gold. He sat down and watched it rise. His hands shook, but the tea helped.

He reran the dream. Fine details he'd never remembered before loomed out. The faces of the men were blurred. As he tried to capture their images in his mind, they faded. He concentrated, but couldn't hold them. He reached for the phone and glanced at the clock, dialed the number and waited.

"San Francisco Police Department, Chinatown Division," a female voice answered. "How may I direct your call?"

"Is Detective Bryson Royo, Homicide, on duty?" he asked.

"Is this an emergency, sir?"

"No," he said.

"Who may I say is calling?"

"If Detective Royo is on duty," he said, "tell him it's Detective Tao Wong."

The dispatcher's demeanor abruptly changed. He heard her mutter "Tao" excitedly under her breath.

"One moment, Detective Wong. Detective Royo is just getting off shift. I'll put you through immediately."

There was silence on the line for a second then a recording with the precinct's menu, then a familiar male voice answered.

"Detective Royo. What can I do for you?"

"Bry, it's Tao. I need some help, buddy."

Chapter 19

Bryson took his feet off of his desk and sat straight, a huge smile lighting his face at the sound of Tao's voice.

"Hey, Tao," he said. "How're you doin'? How's Hong Kong? How's the business? How's Monica? How'd you know I'd be here?"

In spite of the way he felt, Tao smiled. Bryson was the only person in their precinct to take the time to get to know him. They were totally opposite in personality, yet their friendship was a strong one. After the shooting, Bryson and his partner, now wife, Emily Sconey, had come to the hospital and sat by his side the first few days. They had seen him through the rough weeks and months afterwards until he left for New York City with Lee.

"I'm fine," Tao said. "Hong Kong is very busy. The business is doing well. Monica is fine. I forgot about the time difference and got lucky you were there. And I need some information."

Bryson heard the serious tone in Tao's voice and was all business as he grabbed a pen.

"Shoot."

"I need you to look up the file on the death of my parents," Tao said.

The request took Bryson by surprise. He knew how painful and difficult that subject was to Tao.

"Whoa," he said. "I don't know. You know that's off limits to you."

"I wouldn't ask if it wasn't important," Tao said. "I need to know if the killers were ever identified or caught."

Bryson deliberated.

"Well, I can't tell you because I've never seen the files," Bryson said. "I'll see what I can do. It won't be easy. What's going on, Tao?"

"Nothing," he lied. "Nightmares."

Bryson was well acquainted with Tao's nightmares. They had shared the apartment for five years. Many a night he was awakened from a sound sleep by Tao's unexpected shouts. But that alone wouldn't drive Tao to look into the files. They were classified off limits to him because of his relationship to the case, but Tao could get around things like that when he wanted to. Bryson wondered if going to Hong Kong had been such a good idea. The past was something neither of them had given much thought to.

"Oh," he said. "Something surface?"

"Maybe," Tao said. "I remembered something."

"Important?" Bryson asked.

"I'm not sure," Tao said. "It might be, then again, might not. I need to know."

Bryson knew better than to push him. If he wanted Tao to tell, it was better to let him do it when he was ready. Otherwise he'd never find out what it was all about.

"I'll check," he said. "Give me a little bit. I'll have to do some maneuvering to get into the archives. I'll find what I can and overnight the file for you when and if I find something. I make no promises. You know what will happen if I get caught."

There was a long silence then he heard Tao sigh.

"*Dui m jue*," he said. "Sorry. I shouldn't ask. It's just…"

"Look, buddy," Bryson said, "if I didn't want to help, I would tell you. Just expect to pay my bills if I get suspended."

"Deal," Tao agreed.

"Gimme the address," Bryson said.

Tao knew Bryson would do what he could. The file was old and probably buried in the archives of unsolved cases. Also, someone might question why the sudden interest. But Bryson had a way of ferreting out things and kept his mind open to all possibilities that might enable him to do his job more efficiently. He had tucked away little things he picked up in different cases, like the homing device he'd used to track Tao after the shooting. He knew ways to get to information that, if he was found out, would land him in a lot of hot water. Since Tao wasn't exactly orthodox in the way he investigated his cases, he had found Bryson's eccentricities useful.

"You sound tired, buddy," Bryson said. "Are you sure you're okay?"

"Just a headache," Tao said.

Bryson knew about that, too, and about Tao's back. He remembered too well how close Tao came to dying from the injuries sustained in the shooting and the pain he suffered in the aftermath.

"Bad?" he asked.

"No, just an ordinary headache. How's Emily?"

"Expecting," Bryson said.

"*Mat ye a?*" Tao was excited for his friend. "*Gei si a?*"

"Four months to go," Bryson said.

"She isn't working, is she?"

"Not on the beat," Bryson said. "She's working the desk. Her choice. She doesn't want to risk it."

"Good for her," Tao said.

Emily had always seemed levelheaded. Other women in the precinct had worked the beat while they were pregnant. Three of them had lost their babies in violent confrontations.

"Hey, buddy," Bryson said. "We wanted to ask you, and planned to after the baby was born, but how do you feel about being godfather?"

"*Ngoh?*" Tao asked. "Me?"

"Yeah, you," Bryson said.

"I'd be honored," Tao said. "*Doh je.*"

"Oh," Bryson said, "that reminds me. Your foster brother, Joey, called. He told me if I heard from you to tell you to call him. I'd say you'd better do it, too."

"Oh shit," Tao said. "I've been so busy I forgot. Thanks. I better go."

"Okay," Bryson said. "The file will be on its way if you're sure it's what you want."

"Yeah," Tao said.

"Maybe you'll tell me later what this is all about?" Bryson asked.

"Yeah," Tao said, "if I ever figure it out."

They said good-bye and hung up. He went to the kitchen for another cup of tea and heard Lee in his bedroom.

A few minutes later, Lee joined him. He was surprised to find Tao up. Normally it he was the one who did the waking.

"Ready for our run?" he asked.

"Not today," Tao said. "My back hurts."

91

"I thought probably it did," Lee said. "I saw it in your face last night. Lie down on your stomach."

Tao stretched out on the floor of the livingroom. Lee's strong fingers dug into the sore muscles. It was a secure feeling having a paramedic and a nurse in the house. The way things were going, he was liable to need both.

Chapter 20

Ling's subterfuge followed by her husband's declaration distracted Tao. To focus himself and to give Sophie and Lee a chance to get ready for their wedding, he took over some of the more pressing business matters. He volunteered to meet Patrick and his wife at the airport.

Lee was nervous and worried about everything though Kai Chi and Meng had taken care of all the arrangements.

"Just don't leave them stranded somewhere," Lee said.

He was only half joking. Tao and Patrick had butted heads more than once, but maybe Tao would be more affable with Patrick off duty.

Tao drove to the airport early and waited outside the Security gate until he saw Patrick and his wife come through customs. Patrick spied him and waved enthusiastically, hesitated, and lowered his hand with a puzzled frown.

"Tao?" he asked, when he reached him.

Tao nodded as they shook hands.

"You're looking well," Patrick said. "I thought you were Lee. You've filled out."

Tao remembered the last time Patrick had seen him. He was in the hospital recovering. He also remembered that although they'd had differences of opinion during that time, Patrick, when he came to visit Lee in the hospital, hadn't failed to stop in and see how he was doing as well.

"This is my wife, Tina," Patrick introduced the honey blond with blue eyes and a sweet smile at his side.

Tao shook her hand.

"I've heard a lot about you," she said.

Tao flinched.

"Oh don't worry," Patrick said. "I didn't tell her about your kicking me or biting me or anything."

Tina giggled as Tao picked up their luggage and led the way to the car.

"Lee booked you a room at a hotel," he said. "There's an extra room at the apartment, but he thought you might prefer the privacy."

"That was thoughtful," Patrick said. "We would've been happy wherever. I hope the room isn't expensive."

"Uncle Kai insisted," Tao said. "He knows how much it means to Lee to have you here. Price isn't an issue."

"How is Lee really?"

Tao heard the genuine concern in the question. Lee's brush with death had affected the man deeply. The months Lee was in the hospital, Patrick visited almost every day, on and off duty.

"He's doing great," he said. "Most of the time, better than I am."

Patrick gave him a professional scrutiny.

"You seem to be okay," he said.

"Most of the time," Tao said, "but not always."

"How's the new business venture coming?" Patrick asked.

"We're doing fine," Tao said. "Lee's the captain. He loves it."

"I always knew he wanted his own boat," Patrick said. "How about you?"

"I'm happy tinkering with the engines," Tao said. "I like the water. I just wasn't raised on it like he was. I'm more comfortable by myself."

He pulled into a parking space at the docks.

"We thought you'd like to see the yacht," he said.

"Great," Patrick said.

He and Tina followed Tao to the slip and stopped in open-mouthed surprise when they saw the yacht.

"Wow!" Patrick exclaimed.

Lee came out of the cabin, saw them, and waved.

"Ahoy there," he said. "Come aboard."

Patrick helped Tina to the deck and shook hands with Lee. Tina greeted him with a hug. He kissed her cheek.

"This is quite a boat," Patrick said.

"We like it," Lee said. "How was your flight?"

"Long," Patrick said, "and as much as I love seeing you, would you mind if we go to our hotel? We're"

"No problem," Lee said. "Let me lock everything down and I'll go with you."

They drove to the hotel and let Patrick and Tina out in front. Patrick slapped Lee genially on the shoulder.

"You look good, pal," he said. "You're makin' it okay."

"Yeah," Lee said. "We're fine. I got a good coach."

He nodded at Tao.

They promised to get together for dinner the next day. Lee told them where the best places were for sightseeing and said goodbye. As he and Tao drove for home, he nervously cleared his throat.

"Um, we have a charter tomorrow morning," he said.

"What?"

Tao nearly collided with the car in front of him. He quickly corrected his driving and ground his teeth in irritation.

"Tomorrow is Friday. Your wedding is Saturday."

"I know that," Lee said. "It's a morning charter and not going to interfere. We'll be back in plenty of time for the rehearsal."

"What about Sophie?"

"She and Monica have something cooked up, I think," Lee said. "Well, actually I think Mama does. A shower or something tomorrow morning. This call came just before you arrived. Just some businessmen wanting to hold a meeting and do some sightseeing. It'll only be a couple of hours. I didn't see a problem with it."

Tao didn't like it.

"What time?"

"Eight," Lee said. "Early enough we should be home before one."

There wasn't anymore to say. It wasn't worth arguing over so Tao let the matter drop. The charter would keep them both from being nervous.

For reasons of their own, Sophie and Monica thought the charter was a good idea. They were excited about the preparations for the rehearsal and the plans they were making with Meng for the reception. After dinner as they sat on the floor eating popcorn telling Lee and Tao of the plans so far and about the wedding shower Meng was giving Sophie the following morning. They were relaxed and felt better than they had all week.

Monica noticed Tao kept yawning. To her he looked tired and she knew he hadn't been sleeping well. Gently she rubbed his back. He flinched once when she accidentally touched the sensitive area of the damaged nerve. She was glad all the activity of the past few days had encouraged his appetite. Constantly in motion, his body demanded fuel.

He and Lee were up before dawn for their run and workout. They showered, promised to see the girls at 7:00 that evening for the rehearsal, and were at the yacht before 7:00 in the morning. The weather promised to be clear and mild.

Lee was in a good mood and whistled as he worked. The good mood didn't extend to Tao. Something didn't feel right to him. He kept scanning the dock and pier, but no one was there and nothing looked out of place. He checked and rechecked the engines, but nothing was wrong there.

The cars arrived at 8:00. Ten men boarded the yacht. Three of them were dressed in dark business suits and seemed to be in charge. The other seven appeared more like subordinates, or, Tao thought, bodyguards. They were casually dressed in khaki slacks, Hawaiian print shirts, and deck shoes. They wore dark glasses and stood without talking as the business suits sat at one of the tables on deck. Their demeanor immediately set off warning bells. He watched warily them from the cabin as Lee served them coffee and settled them for the cruise. When he returned to the cabin he nodded.

"I know," he said. "Me, too. I felt it the minute they came aboard. I don't like the feel of them."

Tao didn't like it. These weren't ordinary noisy businessmen holding their meeting in the fresh sea air. They shared no camaraderie. They were subdued. Only the main three talked quietly among themselves.

The group made Tao and Lee anxious for the tour to be over. Lee glanced at his watch. It was nearing noon, time to start back to the city.

Tao went below to check the engines. Satisfied all was well there, he stepped onto the deck and felt the barrel of a gun pressed against his temple. He froze.

"Keep coming," one of the men said quietly. "Don't do anything stupid."

Tao moved forward slowly. The gun stayed with him as he was herded to the deck. The other men were armed. Their loose shirts had been perfect for concealing their guns on their belts. He felt the sweat roll down his face as he was walked to the cabin and the door was opened.

Lee turned. When he saw the gun held at Tao's head, icy fear washed over him.

"What do you want?" he asked of the two men who followed Tao inside.

"Just do as you're told," one of them instructed, "and you'll be fine."

He shoved Tao forward. Lee caught him as he stumbled. Both of them faced the men with uncertainty and anger.

"What do you want?" Lee asked again.

One of the main three men stepped to the controls of the yacht.

"You two stay calm and do as you're instructed," he said.

Taking over the instruments, he guided the yacht into open sea.

Chapter 21

Lee glanced at Tao and silently prayed what he feared wouldn't happen.

Tao's face was ashen. His dark eyes filled with deadly anger. His fists clenched at his sides as his body tensed.

Lee caught his attention and shook his head in wordless pleading for him to rein in the fury. With a visible effort, Tao forced his body to relax. Even so, Lee knew it was only a matter of time.

"Boh si," one of the men spoke to the man at the helm, "what do you want to do with these two?"

He waved his gun in their direction. It was a dangerous mistake. Lee grabbed Tao to keep him from attacking. He felt the muscles and tendons like iron cords in Tao's wrist.

"Take them on deck," the man said. "Keep an eye on them."

The man's English was flawless. He wasn't Chinese or even Asian, but his words were heavily accented with what sounded European to Lee. All of the men were a mixture of Asian and other nationalities.

"Who are you?" Lee demanded. "What do you want?"

The man's dark eyes slid in his direction.

"None of your concern," he said. "Get them out."

His man pointed the gun at Tao. Lee held his breath as he felt Tao tense.

"They're here," someone on deck shouted.

Lee heard the approach of another boat and turned to look. For an instant, his hold relaxed on Tao's wrist. Tao took advantage of the diversion. He kicked the gun from the hand of their guard, spun, and landed a second kick to his stomach that sent him crashing into the far wall.

With speed that surprised even him, Lee slammed his hand onto the arm of the leader who cried out in pain and grabbed his now broken wrist. Lee swept the man's legs from under him then brought his fists down hard on his neck.

Tao and the second gunman were locked together, the gun held between them as they fought for control. The gun went off. Instinctively, Lee ducked. He heard excited voices and the sound of feet pounding up the steps to the cabin. He ran forward and grabbed Tao's opponent around the neck. He snapped the man's head back. The man let go of the gun as he and Lee spilled to the floor.

Tao lost his grip on the gun. It skidded across the deck to the door. He started to run for it when the door slid open and several armed men entered, their weapons trained on the cousins.

"Shit!" Tao cursed, breathing hard from his battle as he straightened to face the newcomers.

Lee was shoved away by the man on the floor. They both scrambled to their feet. The other man pushed Lee to where Tao stood as a new arrival entered the cabin.

Lee stared in stunned silence. He noticed, however, that Tao, eyes narrowed and head lowered, wasn't surprised.

Kim's eyes were black as he approached them and viciously backhanded Tao. The blow knocked him to the deck. Lee started forward, but was stopped by the cock of a gun. He looked behind his Uncle into Taibo's sneering face.

Tao climbed to his feet. He ignored his bleeding lip as he straightened in front of his uncle.

Kim was unimpressed.

"Uncle," Lee said, trying to comprehend what was happening. "Who are these people? What's this all about?"

"In time, Lee," Kim said without taking his eyes from Tao. "For now, it's best you not know and do as you are told—both of you."

As Tao held his Uncle's gaze, he spat. Blood and spit landed squarely in Kim's face. With a roar, Kim swung, but Tao ducked the blow and landed two solid punches to his Uncle's chest and abdomen. Kim grunted as he stumbled backwards. Tao moved to strike again.

"Tao!" Taibo said.

He whirled and found Taibo's gun pressed against the back of Lee's head. Lee didn't flinch, didn't move. If Tao continued to resist, he knew both of them would die right there. For Lee, dying was not an option without knowing what was happening or why.

Tao fixed his eyes on Taibo's face. Something slammed into the middle of his back. He fell to his knees with a scream of pain.

Lee started forward.

"Don't," Taibo warned, pressing the gun harder against Lee's skull.

Two gun barrels were aimed directly at Tao's head. Breathing hard against the pain of Tao's fists, Kim backhanded him again.

Lee fought the urge to test what Taibo would do if he moved.

"Taibo," Kim said, "bind him. If he resists, kill Lee."

Lee stared in disbelief at his Uncle, but he knew if Tao fought further, Taibo only needed that excuse to carry out Kim's orders.

Motioning for the men holding Tao to bring him, Taibo led the way to the deck. He threw a rope over a mast and wrapped another around Tao's wrists. He pulled Tao's arms over his head so that he was nearly lifted off his feet.

Taibo stood close to Tao's face and patted his cheek.

"Be a good boy," he jeered, "and you might live."

Tao's answer was to kick him in the chest as hard as he could. Taibo landed on his back on the deck, winded, but was on his feet instantly.

"Watch him," he ordered his men. "If he moves, shoot him."

He tied Tao's ankles to the sail loops anchored in the deck, then hit him hard in the stomach.

Tao's answer was to spit in his face.

"If you're smart," Taibo said as he wiped his face with his sleeve, "you'll curb that nasty habit and stop pushing your luck."

He gripped Tao's chin tightly between the fingers of his right hand. Tao gritted his teeth against the pain.

"And," Taibo said, "Lee's."

He let go.

"I'm going to kill you," Tao said.

Taibo laughed.

"You better take another look, Tao. You're in no position to do anything more than shut your mouth."

Chapter 22

"Why are you doing this?" Lee asked Kim. "What do you want? How did you get here? I don't understand any of this."

"My business matters," Kim said, "require meetings away from prying eyes. I had planned to wait until after your wedding."

He stared out at the ocean. Lee watched and remembered too late the wedding rehearsal. The girls would be waiting for him and Tao.

"Uncle." He made the effort to control the fear in his voice. "We have to be back to Hong Kong tonight. The rehearsal..."

"I know about the rehearsal," Kim said without turning, "but I'm afraid it must be postponed."

He did turn then.

"As will the wedding."

He moved closer to Lee.

"My sources inform me that Tao is prying into matters he shouldn't."

Lee tried to think what Tao might have been doing that he didn't know about. Tao had told him about the phone call to Bryson the morning he had made it, but didn't know why that would upset Kim or how he would know.

"I will give my nephew his due," Kim said, "he is good at his job. Too good. He should have let it go."

Lee had no idea what he was talking about. Kim seemed to think that he did.

"Tao isn't investigating anything," Lee said. "His only inquiry recently was unofficial and only had to—do—with..."

His words faded. Things began to fall into place and he didn't like the picture that was forming.

"Had to do with..."

He swallowed, unable to finish. He couldn't believe it, didn't want to believe it, but suddenly Kim's treatment of Tao from the moment they came face-to-face made sense.

"You!" he said. "It was you!"

He felt sick. His knees weakened under him and he had to lean against the console for support.

"There are things that Tao would be better not knowing," Kim said. "I can no longer take chances."

Lee's confusion and disbelief turned to anger.

"You're afraid he'll find out," he said. "It was you—you who had—Uncle Kong and Aunt Tia—but why? Why? He was your brother!"

"Tao is too much like his father," Kim said. "Kong discovered things about my business he shouldn't have. He used that knowledge against me. I told him it would be best for his family to take a share of the profits. But Kong refused to listen to reason and chose to run away to America. He knew too much. I couldn't chance him telling."

"There's more to it," Lee said. "Tao—the reason you've been so concerned with his being here. He was no threat to you. He doesn't know anything about your business, or care for that matter. There's something else, something you didn't want…"

He stopped as the full realization hit him.

"Be careful, Lee," Kim said. "You're walking a perilous path."

"Am I?" Lee asked. "You're going to kill us both. I'm not stupid. You wouldn't have told me this much otherwise."

"I've told you nothing," Kim said.

"I know the truth!" Lee said. "I know! And you know it, too. You can't let me walk away."

"You don't have to die," Kim said. "The same way that Kong didn't have to die."

"Only Tao, is that it?" Lee asked. "But he doesn't remember. And that's what you're afraid of, that he will remember."

He shook his head.

"If you'd left him alone, he wouldn't have started asking questions. But you pushed and he couldn't let that go. No, you'll have to kill us both, because to leave me alive would be your death warrant."

It was the answer Kim expected. He admired Lee's courage. It saddened him it meant his death as well.

"What is this business?" Lee asked. "You might as well tell me."

Kim smiled and shook his head.

"No, my nephew," he said. "You may find a way to live. I take nothing for granted, not even with Tao. He's survived far too much for me to chance anything. Kong named him wisely. Come with me."

He led the way on deck. Lee followed, accompanied by two of his Uncle's men. There were a dozen more men standing with the *boh si* who had commandeered the yacht. It took monumental effort for Lee to resist going to Tao when he saw him. His anger was hotter than he had ever felt it.

Kim went to Tao.

"If you want to live," he said. "Behave."

Tao struggled against the ropes.

Lee prayed for Tao to be quiet. It was already too late. The ropes dug into Tao's wrists and ankles as he fought against them. Sweat poured from his body. His eyes were brown volcanoes spewing lava.

"I will kill you!" he said.

"You will calm down," Kim said. "You will keep silent and you will do as you are told."

"Nothing you can do can hurt me," Tao said.

"Nothing?" Kim asked. "Taibo, it seems our young Tao needs a lesson."

Taibo took a step toward Tao

"No," Kim said.

He nodded at Lee.

The two men behind Lee grabbed his arms and held him.

"Even better," Taibo said.

. He unwound the long thin braided leather belt from around his waist.

What Lee had mistaken for a metal ornament dangling from the belt was in fact the pommel to which the strap was attached. He struggled but was firmly held by the two men guarding him.

"Turn him," Taibo said.

Lee was jerked around so that his back was to Taibo. Taibo ripped his shirt from his shoulders to his waist, stepped way and swung the strap.

It wrapped around Lee's exposed torso; the sting of it took the breath out of his lungs. The strap left fiery welts up and down his shoulders, chest, arms, and waist.

Tao's jaws ached from his clamped teeth. His arm muscles burned from straining against the ropes as blood ran down his arms and across his chest.

Lee struggled to break free of the hold on him. Tears of anger and pain streamed down his face. After what seemed forever to him, Kim finally ordered Taibo to stop.

Sweating from his efforts, Taibo reluctantly obeyed. He had enjoyed the torture too much. Lee swore if he got the chance, he would repay him for it. He would make Kim pay.

Tao's focus was on his Uncle's face. His breathing was deep, ragged, and barely contained.

"Now, do you understand me?" Kim asked. "You continue to resist…"

He turned to Lee.

"Either of you, and Lee will suffer. Do I make myself clear?"

His answer was an inhuman roar from Tao as he heaved against the rope and snapped it from the moorings. Before Taibo turned completely around, the rope was looped around his neck and he was hauled back against Tao's chest in an iron hold. His ankles bound, Tao crashed to the deck with Taibo on top of him. He held onto the rope, pulled it tighter and tighter to strangle the life out of him. Someone kicked him in the side, but he refused to let go. Taibo gasped for air and tried to pull the rope from his throat.

"Tao!" It was Kim's command.

Tao turned his head. The gun was pressed against Lee's temple.

"Turn him loose or Lee is dead," Kim said.

Taibo felt the rope slacken and rolled away. He coughed and gulped for air as he crawled out of reach. He pulled a knife from his pocket and lunged.

Tao prepared for the attack, but instead of plunging the blade into him, Taibo cut him loose.

"Get up!"

Tao climbed unsteadily to his feet.

"We end this now," Taibo said taking a fighting stance.

"Taibo," Kim said, "enough."

Taibo's attention shifted for a split second to his Uncle and Tao used that moment to surge forward. He closed his hands around the wrist of the hand that held the knife. He heard Lee yell but didn't see Kim swing his arm up. Something hard slammed into the back of his head and he crumpled to the deck.

Lee heard the crack of Tao's skull and saw the blood running from the new gash in the back of his head. He wasn't moving.

"Tao!"

Forgetting his own pain, Lee fought his captors to break free.

"Let me go, damn you!"

Kim looked to his fallen nephew, then to Lee and then to Taibo.

"Throw him overboard," he said, "and take Lee below."

"No!" Lee bellowed.

Taibo lifted Tao over his shoulder and carried him to the rail of the yacht. As he heaved him over the side, Lee finally broke free, ran, and grabbed the folded yellow raft hanging on the rail, flinging it hard into the water only a second before he launched himself from the yacht.

Kim's men began shooting. Bullets ripped past him as he swam to where Tao had gone in. He dove.

"Stop wasting ammunition," Kim ordered. "Taibo, take the helm. Leave them to the ocean."

Taibo nodded and ran to the pilot's cabin. The engines of the yacht roared to life and left Tao and Lee behind.

Chapter 23

Sophie looked at her watch for the third time. She sighed and continued to pace. It was almost 6:00. The rehearsal was at 7:00. Lee and Tao should have been home by 1:00. Monica watched with her.

"Maybe the yacht broke down," she said.

It wasn't the first plausible reason she had offered.

"They have a radio," Sophie said.

Monica tried to think of a reason they might be late; a boat malfunction, a radio problem, the charter extended. No matter how many she came up with, she couldn't let go of the feeling that Tao and Lee weren't alright, that something had gone terribly, horribly wrong on their morning charter.

A knock on the door made them both jump. Sophie hurried to answer it, ready to give Lee a good scolding before hugging his neck and smothering him with kisses. Instead she found Kai Chi, Keung, and Meng standing there and her heart sank.

She and Monica had called Kai Chi when Lee and Tao failed to return on time. He, Keung, and Meng came immediately, reassuring them the men were probably delayed because of their charter wanting extra fishing time or meeting time. Eventually, even they ran out of reasons, especially when numerous attempts to raise the yacht on the radio failed.

Lee and Tao were five hours overdue. With the rehearsal waiting, the previous trouble they had been in for being late without letting the girls know and the lack of radio communication, Kai Chi and Keung had gone to the authorities, friends they knew who wouldn't delay initiating a search for missing persons.

"There's been no word," Kai Chi said. "The last transmission was at noon and they were heading inland. The Harbormaster said nothing seemed wrong. Lee sounded normal and cheerful."

"There's an American Naval carrier," Keung said, "coming through the same corridor they would be in. The Hong Kong Coast Guard has alerted them and asked for their help. They will be watching for the yacht."

"There's nothing we can do," Kai Chi said, "except wait."

They had fought their fears all day, but the two women could no longer ignore the worst. Kai Chi's grave news told them this was indeed a crisis. It was time to face the worst. Lee and Tao were in trouble.

Patrick, Ki, and Chang Wong, two of Keung's sons, searched along the coasts and the tour paths all day. They found nothing and were a quiet group that returned to the docks. Chang slapped Patrick sympathetically on the back.

"Don' worry," he said in his best English. "Lee is good sailor. Water is secon' home to him."

Patrick had joined the search without being asked. No one had objected. The cousins told him they were glad he had come with them. He was impressed by their concern not only for Lee and Tao, but also for him as Lee's friend. They did their best to stay positive, assuring him that Lee was a good sailor, that the yacht was new and in excellent condition, that no matter what it might encounter, Lee could bring it through. They promised they wouldn't stop looking until the yacht and its crew was found.

He climbed into a taxi that took him to his hotel. Tina met him at the door of their suite, her eyes hopeful until she saw his face. She hugged him tightly. In the 10 years the two men had known each other, they had been close. Patrick had helped Lee perfect his English and never begrudged the fact that Lee had made Captain before him. He admired Lee's courage and envied his disregard for his own safety, though on more than one occasion he'd wished he would curb that impulse.

After the fire, after seeing Lee in so much pain, Patrick had cried when he'd left the hospital, finding solace in Tina's arms the rest of the night.

Tina adored Lee's natural shy nature and sweet humor. She'd always thought any woman who captured his heart should consider herself blessed. She'd met Sophie at the hospital and was happy that she had been the one who had finally caught him.

"Nothing at all?" she asked, her face buried in the curve of Patrick's neck.

He held her tightly to him and shook his head, afraid that if he tried to speak, he would break down. She led him to the divan and sat with him.

"They'll find him," she said. "Don't you dare give up on him."

Patrick shook his head.

"I know," he said. "After all he went through, the fire, the months of therapy—Sofia. He defied all the odds. He's happy. This can't be happening."

"Nothing is happening," she said. "We don't know anything is wrong. It may be something mechanical with the yacht. Don't give up."

He buried his face in his hands.

"He's getting married tomorrow."

Tina rocked him.

"It's going to be alright, Pat. You'll see. Lee is resourceful. He's smart. If something happened, he knows what to do in a crisis. He's a trained paramedic and fireman, the same as you. You know he'll be okay."

Patrick didn't say anything. He couldn't.

The silence and the tension in the apartment were affecting all of them. Keung paced back and forth, wracking his brain for anything he might be able to do to find his nephews. Kai Chi stared out of the window at the city below. As a father, Keung understood what Kai Chi must be feeling.

He looked to Meng who was busy in the kitchen fixing soup. She was a strong woman, quiet, but able to remain calm and clearheaded in a crisis. Lee was like his mother in that way.

He remembered Lee as a child, always the watchful eye over the other children, and they listened to him, all except Tao.

Keung smiled at the memory of his youngest brother's son. Tao was adventurous, happy child with a penchant for getting into mischief. The only child of Kong and Tia, he was spoiled by them, and by the rest of the family—with the exception of Kim. Kim wasn't even warm toward his own children. Only with Taibo, his wife's nephew, had he shown anything remotely like affection or attention. There was no reasoning for it.

The phone rang. Keung, closest to it, snatched it up.

"Wei?"

He listened anxiously for a long moment then turned to Monica.

"It's someone named Bryson," he said.

She and Sophie hadn't moved from the couch since his, Kai Chi, and Meng's arrival. There had been no news and the women had at last faced the possibility that something terrible had happened. They had gone into a mild form of shock and Meng had been mothering them since. Wrapped in a blanket, her features haggard, her eyes red from crying, Monica took the phone.

"Bry? It's Nikki."

"What's going on?" Bryson asked. "I asked for Tao. Is he not there? Who answered the phone? Have you been crying?"

She took a deep breath and a firm grip on the phone.

"That was Tao's uncle, Keung. Tao and Lee went out this morning and haven't returned. No one has heard from them."

"What?" Bryson was stunned. "What happened?"

"We don't know," she said. "We don't know yet."

Though she was trying hard, she couldn't keep the break out of her voice. She fought against the tears, but they trickled down her face.

There was a long pause.

"Tao wanted me to check into his parents' deaths," he said, "to see if the killers were ever identified or caught. He didn't tell me why he wanted to know. I have some news for him. Do you want me to tell you?"

Monica didn't have any idea why Tao would be asking about that. He'd said nothing to her about it.

"Nikki?" Bryson said.

"No—I mean—no, talk to his Uncle. I can't—I can't..."

Kai Chi took the phone as Meng took her in her arms as the tears came in force.

"Wei?"

"Mr. Wong?" Bryson said. "My name is Detective Bryson Royo. I don't know if you remember me from the wedding, but..."

"Yes, I remember," Kai Chi said.

"Tao recently asked me to see if the people responsible for his parents' murder were identified or caught," Bryson said. "He didn't say why he wanted to know, but I looked into it for him."

It was unexpected news. Kai Chi was surprised, and apprehensive. He couldn't think what might have prompted Tao to delve into that after all those years, unless he had remembered something. If that was the case, Kai Chi wanted to know what it was.

"What have you discovered, Detective?"

"Two of the killers were identified," Bryson said. "One of them is in prison. The second died in a second robbery shootout with the police. The other two were never found."

Kai Chi straightened.

"Two? There were only three men according to the police who contacted us."

He heard papers rustle on the other end of the line.

"No, four," Bryson said. "One broke into the cash register. He's the one in prison. The dead man is the man who ransacked the store. The driver never left the car and was never identified or captured. The fourth man is the one who shot your brother and your sister-in-law after he raped her. According to the report I found, the police were, and still are, of the opinion that Tao knows who they are, but the trauma of the murders caused him to blank out the memory. He was never able to remember."

He paused for a long moment then said, "Mr. Wong, this is the first time Tao has asked about those files. I think he has remembered something and that worries me."

"Yes," Kai Chi said, in full agreement with the detective's assessment. "Yes. It would seem so. The question is what. Please keep checking. Perhaps the information will solve the mystery of my brother's death for all of us."

Chapter 24

Lee dove as far as his lungs held. He panicked that Tao was already out of his reach. He felt something bump his leg and grabbed Tao's wrist before he slipped away from him. With a strong, one-armed stroke, he swam for the surface, his other arm clasped tightly around Tao's chest.

Lee sputtered and coughed, gulped deep breaths of air. Tao wasn't moving. He turned him face around and held him against his chest. He breathed into his mouth then gently squeezed the air out of him, each time silently encouraging him to breathe on his own.

He felt Tao gag. Water spewed into his face. He continued to squeeze. Each time more water regurgitated until Tao coughed and dragged in air.

With a silent prayer of thanks, he turned Tao onto his back.

Treading water, he looked for the raft. It drifted some distance away. He swam for it. He was tired but was determined not to give up. The water was calm but frigid. Each time he inadvertently swallowed a mouthful, the salt burned his throat.

He reached the bundled raft with an effort and draped his free arm over it to give himself a moment of rest. He looked at Tao face. Tao's mouth was tinged with blue, but he was breathing. Lee knew hypothermia was setting in. He had to get both of them out of the water quickly.

He wrapped his legs around Tao to hold him in place, as he pulled the cord to inflate the raft. He held on tight so it wouldn't slip out of his grasp. It was a struggle, but he managed to heave Tao to the side and over. He shoved him from the hips and he tumbled in.

The raft bumped him and almost knocked him loose. He clung to it, long enough to scramble over the edge. By the time he was inside, he wheezed and was covered in sweat as well as water, a very bad combination. Too tired to do, he lay down next to Tao and passed out.

Tao didn't lose consciousness after being hit on the skull, but the shock of the blow temporarily paralyzed him. He heard Taibo's nasty laugh as he was lifted and tossed over the side of the yacht. Hitting the water added to his shock. His instinct was to swim, but his body refused to respond to the screaming commands of his brain. As he sank, water flooded his nose, throat, and lungs as it closed over his head. He was aware of every sensation yet helpless to fight against it. He drifted in and out of shadows, weightless, until he felt the cold air on his face, the warm breath in his mouth and nose that tasted of peppermint and coffee. Three times, four, five, six, each time the air was squeezed out of him. His body at last responded. Water surged from him, burned his throat and mouth. There was a pressure on his skin, a soothing voice, motion, then silence.

Lee woke to the sound of thunder. He rolled onto his back and looked directly into the roiling black sky. He remembered what had happened and sat up too quickly. He threw up over the side of the raft.

The wind picked up, tossed the raft like a cork on the ever-increasing waves. He pulled Tao into his arms and felt for a pulse. There was a strong one. He sighed in relief. He couldn't tell if Tao was unconscious or not. He patted his cheeks and spoke to him, but there was no response.

He looked at his watch that miraculously had stayed on his wrist. It was nearly 6:00. They had been on the raft five hours, too long.

Gently he probed the back of Tao's head. He found the new gash. It was deep, but he didn't see bone. That was good. It would need stitches. He tore the hem of what was left of his shirt and wrapped the strip of cloth around the injury. He rubbed Tao's hands and chest to get the circulation going. He spoke to him and gently shook him. At last Tao responded with a moan and tossed his hands fitfully.

A loud crack of thunder made him jump. He looked up. The sky was ebony. Lightning streaked to the water. The wind howled. The raft was picked up and thrown from wave to wave like a cork. There was nothing he could do but hold onto Tao and pray for survival.

The rain came in solid sheets. The welts on his back stung as the water hit them. He stretched himself and Tao full length to distribute their weight evenly and lessen the chance of capsizing.

It didn't take long before he realized the raft was filling with water. At first it worried him, then he reasoned the water would be fresh. He scooped it into the cup of his palm and gingerly tasted it. There was a slight saltiness to it, but it was fresh enough to drink. If the raft didn't flood or capsize, they would have drinking water for a day at least before it evaporated.

Totally helpless to do anything but stay in the raft, he lay still and prayed.

A blast shook Tao. Again water was in his face. He tried to ward it away with his arms, but they wouldn't obey him. Wild motion tossed and threw him, spinning, falling, jolting as piercing howls and explosions filled his ears. He wanted to scream, to beg the noise to stop. Again the soothing voice came in words he didn't understand. He wanted to open his eyes, but couldn't. He wanted to move but was unable to make his body obey. It made him angry. He felt his fingers curl like claws unsheathed. That small movement gave him courage.

It was morning when Lee woke again. Still soaked, he sat up and looked around. The sky was clear and the air warm. He shifted his back and the movement broke open the welts, allowing the crusted salt into the wounds. He clenched his teeth against the sting. Fortunately it only lasted a minute.

He examined Tao. The blue was gone and his face had more color.

Lee cupped his hand into the water caught in the bottom of the raft and held some to Tao's lips. Tao's eyes opened. Lee thought he detected a touch of fever in them and felt of his forehead. He was hot, but from fever or the sun, it was hard to know for certain.

He settled against the side of the raft and cradled Tao's head on his lap. Tao muttered something he didn't understand. Lee offered him another drink, but he shook his head.

"What time—is it?"

Lee looked at his watch. It was almost 11:00, his wedding day.

"I'm sorry, Sophie," he whispered. "Forgive me."

He buried his face in Tao's hair. There would be no wedding, but in his heart, he said the vows he would somehow, someday find a way to share with the woman he loved.

Tao heard the soft weeping. The sound broke his heart and fueled his determination to find his uncle.

Sophie stood by the window in the apartment and stared across the city to the ocean and whispered "I love you" to Lee. She slipped the wedding ring on her left finger and said her vows to herself. Behind her she heard Kai Chi, Keung, Chang, Ki, and Patrick in earnest conversation. They'd been out all night on Keung's boat, but had been driven in by the storm. The Coast Guard called early to report there was still no sighting of the yacht, but the American Naval carrier had launched two reconnaissance planes to search. The chance of finding Lee and Tao was improved by that cooperation.

Bryson spoke for an hour with Kai Chi concerning the file on Kong and Tia's deaths. Tao's silence those first few months had allowed two of the killers to escape. When Bryson gave Kai Chi the name of the man in prison, Kai Chi knew where the others had escaped to and why Tao was such a threat to Kim.

Tao didn't know, didn't remember the face of the man Monica confirmed Tao had said he saw. That one memory was not only the key, but the answer to the mystery.

In private, Kai Chi confided what he'd been told to Keung. To his surprise, Keung didn't object or argue. He knew things Kai Chi didn't and confessed he'd suspected the truth for years. They had to find Lee and Tao, dead or alive. Once that was accomplished, Kai Chi and Keung would finish the matter by finding the man responsible, the man Tao saw rape and murder his mother.

Chapter 25

Something jolted the raft and someone touched Lee. Weakly, he tried to open his eyes and brush the hand away.

"Take it easy." The voice was deep, male, and American. "We've gotcha. You're gonna be okay now."

"Huh?" Lee forced his eyes into slits.

A man in a black wet suit leaned over him. The man was talking to someone else in the other end of the raft and there was the sound of clinking metal and a loud whir that stirred the water into a fine cold spray that hit Lee in the face.

Lee tried to sit up to see what was going on.

"No, now," the man said, "just hold on."

There was another clink of metal and something was clasped around Lee's chest and shoulders.

"Okay," the man said into a radio in his hand. "This one's ready. Take him up."

Lee fet a tug and was lifted from the raft into the air. He looked down and caught a momentary glimpse of Tao being settled into a harness. A minute later, Lee was pulled into the helicopter that hovered over the water like a giant dragonfly, and placed in a rescue basket before being stripped of his wet clothes and wrapped in blankets.

"Gonna be a sting," someone said, and Lee felt a needle prick his left arm.

"It's okay," the same person spoke again. "It's just fluids."

Lee was beginning to realize the persons around him were American military medics. They were quick, efficient, and amazingly gentle as they worked.

He felt a bump and heard a scrape. The medics spoke in rapid succession, their words running together until he barely understood them. He turned his head and saw Tao hoisted into the helicopter and placed in a second rescue basket.

One of the medics bent over him examining the head injury.

"Stitches," the medic shouted over the roar of the whirling blades of the helicopter now carrying them over the water, away from the tiny raft left bobbing like a tiny cork in the ocean.

There was general scrambling of feet and movement around Lee and Tao. Lee heard one of the medics ask Tao a question. He heard Tao answer, but couldn't understand what he said. He was tired and unable to hold his eyes open any longer, he drifted off to sleep.

Tao had awakened when the shadow of the military helicopter had fallen over the raft. At first unable to see anything but a huge black shape above him, he'd been frightened until he realized what it was. Several bodies dropped into the water and then climbed into the raft on each end. He identified their wet suits. He wanted to say something to the man on his end, but couldn't get his mouth to work. The noise of the helicopter hurt his hears and pierced his already throbbing head.

"Lee," he said, but even he wasn't sure he'd said it out loud. He didn't hear any sound come out of his mouth.

"Don't you worry," the man in the wet suit said, "we're taking you out of here."

The harness was clasped around him and he was lifted into the air. As soon as he reached the hatch on the big bird's side, he was settled into a rescue basket, his clothes removed and blankets wrapped around his shivering body. Something stuck his arm and the back of his head. He heard the word 'stitches' as his mind began to shut down. He waged an internal struggled not to lose consciousness, but lost the battle.

He stood in the sunshine by a gate leading to a well-manicured yard and stone house. Monica smiled as she watched a toddling baby with thick black hair playing among colorful flowers in a tidy Chinese garden. It confused him. He and Monica had no child.

A hand touched his shoulder and he turned. Ling stood behind him, a thin, pale, ragged caricature holding the hand of an emaciated, sunken eyed boy. In Ling's ghost white face, her glowing crimson eyes were filled with hate. She hissed at him, like a cat. He stumbled away from her as a dagger flashed in her upraised hand.

Her face changed, replaced by the cadaverous face of Sonja, who had once stalked him, begging him to love her. She drove the dagger deep into his abdomen. He grabbed the hilt. Blood poured from the wound. He turned for Monica, but she was unaware of anything but the garden and the child.

He stood in an empty street, hearing gunshots. He felt bullets wind their horrible paths through his body and saw the blood stain his shirt scarlet. He turned his head.

His father smiled down at him as they stacked the boxes in the storeroom. Weakly he returned the smile, even though the dagger still protruded from him and blood trickled down his neck. There were angry voices somewhere and Kong ran from the storeroom to a room filled with bright white light.

Tao stumbled after him, and as he reached the light, the world turned gray and colorless. His father lay in a growing pool of blood, dead eyes staring at the ceiling.

Tia, lying on the floor and being smothered by the hulking man on her, found her son's face. There was terror in her eyes as she drew sharp nails across the man's face, leaving deep scarlet gashes on his cheek.

"Run!"

The man holding her shot her in the face. He and Tao's eyes met. A door shattered in Tao's mind, made him jump as for the first time, he clearly saw the face of the killer and knew it.

Keung hurried to the deck after he signed off the radio. He and the others had been searching all morning when he received the transmission from the Harbormaster and his relief was overwhelming.

"They found them," he said, smiling a rare broad smile. "The Naval carrier found a raft. Tao and Lee were in it. They'll be rendezvousing with the Coast Guard in the morning."

Kai Chi breathed a heavy sigh of relief.

"Are they alright?" he asked.

"I don't know," Keung said. "The Harbormaster had no specific details.

But they are found, Dai Goh, and that's all that matters."

Kai Chi smiled in spite of his worry. He'd never seen his younger brother elated by anything. Keung's joy and relief literally danced on his face. It was an amazing sight and Kai Chi felt the same.

Patrick, standing next to Kai Chi, closed his eyes and said a silent prayer of thanks. At least they were found and, as Keung said, that was all that mattered.

"Ba ba," Chang called to Keung from the cockpit, "It is the HKHP."

Keung hurried back to his radio, followed closely by his brother and Patrick. They wanted to hear any further news themselves.

"The Commander of the American Naval Carrier has just informed us that both men are alive," the voice on the other end of the radio informed them. "They are suffering from mild hypothermia and dehydration, but their conditions are good and stable. The Coast Guard is sending an air ambulance to pick them up and take them straight to the hospital."

"Good," Keung said. "We are on our way in. We should arrive just before they do. Thank you for your assistance in this emergency. Out."

He looked to his brother. This time his expression was dire. Now that he knew his nephews were alive and safe, he let his worry turn to anger.

"Who did this?" It was Ki who spoke. "Why, Ba ba? And what happen to the yacht?"

"There's a lot of questions needing answers," Patrick said. "I for one want to know what those answers are."

The other men agreed. Kai Chi and Keung felt they already knew, but they needed proof.

Keung placed a ship to shore call to the apartment and told Meng the news.

Meng placed the phone on the table and turned to Monica and Sophie. Both women were in their bathrobes, sitting on the couch, their faces pale and eyes red and swollen from crying. Uneaten toast and cold cups of tea sat on the coffee table. Neither woman had slept more than a couple of hours in the past two days.

"Tao and Lee are found," Meng informed them. "They are safe. The Coast Guard is taking them to hospital. Keung said they need rest."

She held Monica and Sophie tight as they hugged her, crying for joy.

"Oh thank God," Sophie said against Meng's shoulder.

"Come," Meng said as she pulled gently away and held them at arm's length. "It will be tomorrow before they arrive. You need to sleep. So do I, if we are to be presentable when we go to hospital.

She got them off to bed and watched with gratification as they promptly fell into a deep, restful sleep. She gathered the dishes and carried them to the kitchen, then set an alarm clock from Monica's room before curling onto the couch with a comforter and falling asleep.

Chapter 26

Something hissed in Tao's ears, a sound he recognized. He experienced a terrifying moment just before waking from a dream about the shooting in San Francisco. The light around him was soft, the air cold, but not uncomfortable. He was in the hospital and he remembered why. Delicate fingers brushed his hair from his forehead. Monica lovingly kissed his cheek.

"Welcome back, love," she whispered.

"It was a close call," the doctor said later as they gathered around Tao's bed.

He was sitting up, fully awake, with Monica's hand held tightly in his.

Lee sat in the bed next to Tao's. Sophie stood protectively by him.

Kai Chi, Meng, Keung, and Patrick waited to hear what the doctor had to say.

"In essence," the doctor said, "the salt caused an infection in Tao's left lung. X-rays show that lung isn't as strong as it should be. It amazes me that the two of you aren't in worse straits."

Tao managed a smile he didn't feel and shifted uncomfortably against the upraised bed. He ached all over. His wrists and ankles were still raw from the rope burns.

Lee remained grim and silent. Everytime he tried to move, the thin welts and bruises on his back made him wince. The doctor had him lean forward so he could examine the damage.

"I'll give you something to ease the pain a little. I don't want to give you too much though. It's best if you don't get used to pain killers."

"Tao has some at the apartment," Monica said. "They're for his back."

"Do you know what they are?" the doctor asked.

She told him and he wrote it down.

"He should be able to take them as well. I'll have some brought to both of them. In the meantime, massage Lee's back with menthol. The bruises are healing."

He shook his head.

"I've never seen anything like this."

He turned to Kai Chi.

"Is there any word from the authorities?"

"No," Kai Chi said. "We have some of the names from the appointment log, but they aren't Chinese. The names may not be real. We have no idea where they came from or what they were doing."

"Or where they went," Keung said.

His anger was visible in his sober expression. As did Kai Chi, he hovered protectively near his nephews until they were in no more danger.

Lee had told them and the authorities that the men who took over the yacht had tried to kill him and Tao. He hadn't told them who was behind the hijacking. When he had time alone with Tao, he would discuss it with him and make plans to settle the score. For the first time he felt the blood of the tiger stirring in his veins. He understood Tao more than he ever had.

In his entire life, he had never felt vengeful against anyone. Even Arturo Gravelli hadn't aroused so much blood anger in him. Kim was family, the head of the family. What he'd done was unforgivable. And what Lee would tell Tao wouldn't be easy, but Tao had to know the truth.

Lee insisted that Sophie and Monica go home with Meng and Kai Chi. He wanted time alone to talk with Tao and, not knowing what Kim might do, he felt more secure knowing they weren't alone in the apartment.

The pain pills had been delivered. Tao leaned against his pillows feeling less pulverized. He watched Lee, suspecting that he wanted to tell him something.

"I need to talk to you," Lee said. "I know what this is all about and why."

"So do I," Tao said. "I saw his face the night Mama and Ba ba were killed. I remembered. Just before I woke up, I saw his face. I understand everything. What I don't understand is why he murdered them."

Lee only knew what Kim had told him. He hadn't realized that Kim had participated personally in the murders. He closed his eyes agasint the sudden dizziness and leaned back into his pillows until it passed.

"Uncle Kong knew what Uncle Kim was doing," Lee said. "He admitted that much to me after Taibo took you on deck. He said Uncle Kong discovered information he shouldn't have. He never told, but was afraid to stay in Hong Kong. I don't know what Kim's business is. He wouldn't say, but if he kills to keep it secret, it's bad, very bad."

"That's why we moved?" Tao asked.

"It seems so," Lee said.

"But it wasn't enough," Tao said.

"Kim was afraid of whatever Kong knew," Lee said. "Kim didn't want to leave anything to chance."

"So he murdered my family, his own brother," Tao said, his fists clenched in the sheets.

"I think," Lee said, "that he intended to kill all of you. My guess is that he wanted it to look like a random gang killing. Let's face it, who's going to look twice at newly arrrived immigrants in a gang crossfire."

Tao had to concede that point. As a San Francisco cop he had been to many such scenes.

"What he didn't count on was your escape," Lee said, "but he didn't worry about it after he heard you had vanished. He was in Hong Kong, safe. You were a traumatized little boy who didn't speak or understand English. Baba gave up trying to locate you. Uncle Keung had no better luck. Kim wasn't going to bother."

He shook his head at the irony of it all.

"When you went to China, he didn't go to the ceremony because he was afraid you'd recognize him. When you arrived in Hong Kong then, you didn't recognize him. That's why he wanted you to go. He made sure you would."

He glanced at the silent Tao, who was listening.

"He didn't count on you returning to Hong Kong. When you did, he worried what you might remember. So he set Taibo on you or let him conduct his own private hate campaign to make you angry and force you back to the States, but it didn't work."

Lee shook his head incredulous at the whole thing. It was all conjecture on his part, but he had the feeling he was close if not right on target about it.

"You're a liability. He had to kill you. But he didn't count on anyone getting in the way. Now there's the two of us. He can't leave me alive after what he told me."

"He thinks we're dead," Tao said.

Lee nodded.

"And that's to our advantage," he said.

Lee's theory made sense to Tao—the animosity, the accusations—Kim had sent Ling with her story in hopes he would be shamed into leaving. It had backfired. Kim underestimated him on every point. He was tenacious, stubborn, and secretive. He pushed when retreat would be wiser. He refused to let go long after everyone else gave up. Those were the traits that had made him the detective he had been. It was why he'd survived what would've killed most men. When he set on a trail, he kept coming, more and more fierce until he, at last, cornered his prey.

Lee knew as soon as Tao was on his feet, he would be hunting their Uncle. It wouldn't matter how long. Tao wouldn't give up. Sooner or later, Kim would turn around and find the Tiger behind him. There would be no escape. When that time came, Lee intended that Tao wouldn't stand alone.

Chapter 27

After three days in the hospital, Lee and Tao went home depressed. The whereabouts of the yacht was still unknown. Without it there was no business.

Kai Chi insisted they use the time to rest and regroup. There was still the wedding to be held as soon as Lee felt up to it.

He felt guilty about the postponement and apologized profusely to Sophie as soon as they were alone. It was his fault, he told her, that they had taken the charter the day they were hijacked. She assured him she didn't blame him. She was angry, but at the circumstances and the people responsible. She showed him that she wore the wedding ring. No matter what, as far as she was concerned, they were husband and wife.

When they made love that night, he knew he loved her more than he could've thought possible. As she lay sleeping in his arms, he said a silent prayer of thanks for this woman. He knew he and Sofia would never have had the life he'd found with Sophie. There was peace with her. All the things that happened worked out the best for him.

He offered one more silent prayer. This one for his tragic Sofia that she had found the peace and love he had.

He kissed Sophie and pulled her tighter against him, grateful to be alive to do so. He came too close to losing her forever. She stirred. Her hand found the place on his chest where the beat of his heart was strong.

"Why are you so pensive tonight?" she asked.

"I was just thinking how much I love you," he said.

She laid her cheek on his shoulder.

"Let's have a quiet ceremony," she said. "Just the family and Patrick. I don't need a fancy wedding."

"What about your gown, the tuxes?" he asked.

"We can still wear them," she said, "but on Kai Chi's boat, on the ocean."
Lee shifted so he could see her face.

"I know Kai Chi will be disappointed," she said. "He worked so hard and spent so much to decorate the garden, but it's what I want."

"After what just happened?" he asked.

"Especially after that," she said. "To defy the sea, let it know you belong to me and no one else."

He kissed her. She continued to amaze him.

"I'll talk to Ba ba."

Kai Chi wasn't happy, but with a little prodding from Meng, he agreed to the change of plans.

The date was reset. They held a combination welcome home, pre-wedding dinner two weeks after the rescue. During the dinner, Kai Chi presented Lee with his wedding gift. Lee opened the small package and found a wooden box with a gold key inside.

"At your Slip," Kai Chi said. "From your mother, me, and your Uncle Keung."

"A new yacht?"

"New to you," Kai Chi said. "I'm afraid, at such short notice it had to be previously owned, but it's in excellent condition. I had it thoroughly inspected. You can't give tours without a way to conduct them."

Lee turned to Tao who smiled for the first time since the hijacking.

Recovery had taken longer for him. The knowledge that he was meant to die, and now the knowledge of why, bothered him. He told Monica what he'd discovered, but made her swear to tell no one else. She stood fiercely by him, but was concerned about what he might do. Remembering what had happened with Arturo Gravelli, she worried that Tao would go after his uncle and the final confrontation could be as dangerous and as deadly. She decided it might not have been in his best interest to return to Hong Kong. When he was ready, she intended to try and talk him into returning to the States, somewhere there were no memoires for either of them to face.

"We can hold the wedding onboard," Kai Chi said. "I've made all the arrangements. This will be a proper christening for the yacht."

Lee and Tao were ready after two weeks of agonizing over how they would replace the yacht. Everything they owned was tied in their business. It had just started to make a profit. The hijacking had set them back in more ways than one. They knew if they didn't restart soon, they would lose everything. The gift couldn't have come at a better time.

Drinks were served. Keung stood to make a toast. Just as he raised his glass, the house manager hurried in, a look of distress on her face as she spoke softly to Kai Chi. He came to his feet just as an extremely thin woman with a haggared and sallow face, and dull gray hair that looked as lifeless as straw and covered her head like a close fitting hat, stormed into the room. Her dark eyes were rat-like, small and gleaming with malice. Behind her followed three young men.

"Palau," Kai Chi said. "What is the meaning of this?"

"Where is my husband?" she demanded in a voice that screeched like chalk on a chalkboard.

She pointed a long bony finger at Kai Chi.

"Two weeks he has been missing. You haven't looked for him. It's your place to find what's become of him."

"Two weeks?" Keung asked. "Kim has been missing for two weeks and you're just now telling us? Why haven't you come before now?"

"He was on business," Palau said, "with Lee on his yacht. Lee is here, but the yacht and Kim are missing."

Kai Chi and Keung looked at the cousins.

"Kim was on that yacht?" Kai Chi asked.

"No," Lee said. "He wasn't onboard."

He glanced at Tao. They had sworn not to let that information get out.

Kai Chi saw the exchange.

"Lee," he said. "The truth."

"It is the truth," Lee said. "He wasn't onboard with the charter. We rendezvoused with another boat. Kim and Taibo were on it. Uncle Kim was behind the hijacking."

Sophie went to him.

Monica turned to Tao who sat rigidly staring at his still full plate. He hadn't eaten well since the rescue. She'd pleaded for him to tell Kai Chi what he'd told her. She was glad it was in the open.

"You lie," Palau said. "He was on that yacht and didn't come back. You killed him. You sank the boat and killed him and my nephew, then pretended to have been thrown overboard."

She turned her anger on Tao.

"Since you came here, you've caused nothing but trouble for your Uncle. You hated him. Now he's gone and here you are. You killed him. I know it."

Her accusations were more than Lee could stand.

"We didn't kill him and you know that, Palau. But, if we ever get our hands on him…"

"Lee!" Keung said.

Lee ignored him.

"He meant to kill us. He was the one who ordered me beaten so Tao wouldn't fight him. He's the one who hit Tao over the head and had him thrown overboard."

Monica held tightly to Tao's hand.

"Kim offered to spare my life," Lee said, "but he wanted Tao dead. He hates Tao because he's afraid of what he knows."

Sophie wrapped her arms around him. She felt his whole body quake.

"Tao didn't know," Lee said. "but he knows now. If Kim comes near either of us again…"

He knew what he wanted to say, but for the sake of his father, he didn't say it.

"Family and honor come first," he said.

It was clear enough what he meant. No one said a word. Kai Chi looked to Keung who stood rigid and angry. He turned to Tao.

"Tao," Keung asked, "who killed your parents?"

Tao raised his head. His eyes met his Uncle's and Keung could see he didn't want to answer.

"What?" Tao asked.

Keung moved to his side and placed his hands on his shoulders.

"I know this is painful for you," he said. "But I believe you know now. Who killed Kong and Tia?"

Everyone waited.

Tao looked to Monica for guidance.

"Tell them the truth," she said.

"Ba ba knew—something," he said. "Whatever it was, he left Hong Kong so he didn't have to face it. But it wasn't enough."

He took a deep ragged breath and looked directly at Palau.

"Kim killed them," he said. "I saw him."

"You lie!" Palau screamed. "How can you dishonor your Uncle with such lies?"

"Be quiet," Kai Chi ordered. "Listen or leave."

"I will not stay and have my husband maligned," she said. "If he's not home soon, my sons will return."

Keung fingers tightened on Tao's shoulders as the three young men standing with Palau gathered close around her.

"If you or your sons come near Lee or Tao," he said, "you'll lose more than your husband."

"You would turn on your own brother for that?" Palau said, pointing at Tao.

"I would turn on him because he is a cold-blooded killer," Keung said. "I loved my brother and I will protect his son. Wherever Kim is he is well advised to stay there. He's no longer welcome here."

"Get out, Palau," Kai Chi ordered. "And don't come back."

Brusquely she turned on her heels and stalked out. Her sons followed. Keung turned to Tao.

"Tell us what you remember," Keung said.

Tao felt sick. He didn't want to remember. The dreams had opened all the closed doors. He wanted to shut them again because remembering hurt too much.

"Tao."

Lee's gentle voice spoke at his elbow. He felt Lee's hand on his arm. Without looking up, he told them what he'd remembered. When he finished, he turned to Kai Chi.

"If he had left me alone—but he didn't! Why didn't he leave me alone!"

Meng went to comfort him. She sat in the chair next to his and held his hand.

"What can he be doing that he would murder his own family to protect?" she asked.

Kai Chi turned to Keung.

"What do you know? You've known something all along. It's time to end all the secrecy. It's past time."

"I can't say for certain," Keung said. "I've known for years his money didn't come from the family business. Even before Ba ba died, Kim was running his own operation. Ba ba knew and was working with the authorities. I found this out shortly after he died. I was ordered to say nothing. If Ba ba hadn't died when he did, he would've stopped Kim."

"Do you think…" Meng started to say, but what she was thinking was too horrible.

Her father-in-law had died suddenly in what had been ruled an accident. Now she wondered.

Kai Chi understood.

"Is it possible?" he asked.

"We'll never know," Keung said. "As far as the authorities were concerned Ba ba's death was an accident. I have friends in sensitive positions that have provided me with information on Kim. The authorities are watching him. He's probably aware of it. We are working with the U.S. government because we believe Kim is now providing North Korea with stolen nuclear plans. We've no proof, but it's only a matter of time."

He placed his hand on Tao's head and felt the outline of the scar.

"If you hadn't returned, Kim would still be in the open. He's hemmed himself in by attacking you. You didn't know, but now you do and you've survived. You and Lee must be very careful. Until Kim is brought to justice, it's dangerous for both of you."

Chapter 28

Because of the media coverage of the rescue at sea, Keung and Kai Chi secreted several crates of weapons on the yacht where they would easily be accessed. Alert to the possibility of trouble during the wedding, they enscripted several Wong cousins as members of the crew, telling Lee and they were just temporary help as servers and ushers. Kai Chi didn't want to cast a shadow over what should be a day of joy for his son, but he wasn't taking any chances.

Tao and Monica did their part for the wedding by spending an entire day polishing and cleaning the yacht. They were joined by other family members secretly acting as bodyguards.

The weather for the wedding dawned clear and warm. Meng saw to the decorations, flowers, and ribbons.

The yacht set out at 10:00 and set anchor an hour later. At noon, Ki started the recorded music. Kai Chi led Sophie in her white gown to Lee's side.

Tao, the best man, winked at Monica in her place as Matron-of-Honor. She smiled as she held the bouquets while Lee and Sophie joined hands and repeated their vows.

The guests, consisting mostly of aunts, uncles, cousins, and two of Lee's three brothers who managed to fly in for the wedding, hugged Sophie in welcome to the family and shook Lee's hand in congratulations.

The professional photographer was busy taking pictures. The reception was set up on the top deck. Lee held Sophie close as the music began and whirled her in her gown and veil that floated about her like an angel's wings.

After the first dance, the cake was cut, and Patrick called everyone to attention as he raised his glass to propose a toast. The glass shattered. A second later the sound of gunshots echoed across the water.

Startled, he dropped the remains of the glass and ducked. Chang shouted to his father that a boat was approaching the yacht at high speed and the men onboard had guns.

"Get the women inside," Kai Chi ordered.

Meng, her two older sons, and Monica herded the frightened women and children into the staterooms and told them to lie facedown on the floor.

Keung flung open the lockers and threw the men on deck the high powered rifles. More gunfire ripped into the yacht.

Tao, an expert sharpshooter, took out the engine on the oncoming boat. It smoked and sputtered to a stop several yards away.

Kai Chi shouted into a cell phone for help. A bullet pinged off the rail near his head. He went to his stomach

The men on the disabled boat could do little more than take chunks out of the yacht. Tao heard the sound first. He scanned the sky and finally spied the approaching helicopter.

"Lee," he shouted, "can you get us moving?"

Lee slid like a lizard across the deck on his hands and toes, hunched at the bottom of the steps and watched Tao. Tao counted to three, then shouted "Go!"

He stepped into the open and let loose a volley of gunfire, giving Lee the cover to get to the helm. The engines fired to life. The anchor began its ascent even as Lee pushed the throttle forward. They began to move, but the older yacht was sluggish.

The helicopter gained on them. In the distance, another smaller boat came at them in full speed.

Tao took his rifle and a box of ammunition to the second deck behind the helm. Aiming carefully, he fired several rounds at the helicopter, shattering the windshield. He saw one man slump to the side. The helicopter was directly over them. The other boat was still some distance away. The yacht was pinned down. It didn't possess the power needed to outrun the attack.

A bullet ripped into the helm and sliced a path through Lee's right arm. He yelped as he fought to bring the yacht around. If he could coax the yacht to move, he intended to ram the other boat.

Tao fired several shots into the helicopter. One of the men inside fell from it into the water.

There was a cry of pain from the deck. Ki fell facedown and didn't move again. There were other cries of pain as some of the men were wounded. Tao knew they needed help and soon. He hoped his Uncle's call had gotten through.

The other boat arrived, swung to the left, and one of the men on it threw a grenade that landed on the deck of the yacht. Tao launched himself from his perch, grabbed the grenade and heaved it with all of his might over the side. It exploded in mid-air as he was forced by gunfire to duck.

Another grenade landed, this time close to where Kai Chi and Chang were concealed. Before Chang could react, Kai Chi grabbed the grenade and stood to throw it.

"No!" Tao shouted, scrambling to his feet.

Just as the grenade left Kai Chi's hand, bullets tore into him. The grenade landed near the stern of the yacht. The explosion rocked them. The engines coughed to a stop.

With a bellow of grief, Tao caught his uncle and cradled him, tears of rage streaming down his face. He knew there was nothing he could do for him.

"Tao, watch out!" Patrick shouted.

Tao saw the incoming grenade. With superhuman speed and reflexes, he caught the grenade and launched it at the helicopter. The exploding helicopter dropped into the ocean, its rotor slicing through the middle of the immobilized boat. Fire ignited leaking fuel and the boat went up in a ball of orange flame.

Patrick, on his way to Kai Chi, stopped in his tracks unable to believe what he'd just witnessed. He'd never seen anyone move like that. A second later he was diving to cover to avoid the bullets from the second boat.

Two more boats were approaching, sirens blaring. The other boat arched and took off at high speed. One of the Harbor Patrol went after it. The other pulled alongside the yacht. Help had come at last, too late.

During the battle, the women hovered over their children and clung to each other. Monica and Sophie shielded Meng with their bodies as best they could as every explosion brought screaming and crying from the women and children.

In the silence that followed, they were too afraid to move. Then slowly, cautiously, they began to stand and huddle close to each other as the door opened and they saw the devastation on deck.

Lee ran from the helm to the deck. Patrick grabbed him, attempting to keep him from seeing Kai Chi, but he jerked away and stumbled to his knees by his father's side and pulled the lifeless body into his arms.

"Ba ba," he wept, burying his face in Kai Chi's hair, "Ba ba, *dui m jue.*"

Woodenly, Tao knelt next to him, feeling as if he'd lost his father all over again.

"It's not your fault, Lee," he whispered.

He sandwiched Kai Chi's hand between his. He felt weak and sick—and dangerously angry.

"If we'd had the wedding in the garden…" Lee said.

"The attack would've come in the garden," Tao said.

He had no doubts. The attack was meant to happen any place they decided to have the wedding. Kim was determined to kill them all.

"Kai Chi!"

Meng ran forward. One of her sons tried to stop her, but she shoved him away and sank to the deck next to her husband. Her sons knelt with her and held her as her grief took over. Lee's tears mingled with his mother's on Kai Chi's lifeless face.

Tao rose and let his gaze drift to Chang, his sisters, and Keung who cradled Ki's body to him. He turned away and walked to the rail of the yacht where he stared out at the sea. All of this had happened because he had returned to Hong Kong. He had to undo it, and he knew of only one way— he had to find Kim and Taibo.

Chapter 29

The phone rang six times before Bryson picked it up. He glanced at the clock. It was 2:00 in the morning. There was only one person he knew who would call him at that hour.

"What's up, Tao?" he asked, his voice husky with sleep.

"I need that information," Tao said. "All information you can find on the death of my parents."

"Good morning to you, too," Bryson said.

There was a long pause.

"Dui m jue," Tao said at last. *"Jo san.* Good morning. I'm sorry I woke you, but this is important."

Bryson detected anxiety in Tao's voice. Something was wrong. He'd been worried about Tao every since he asked for the files.

"Tao, I don't know about you delving into that," he said.

"Uncle Kai Chi has been killed," Tao said. "Yesterday, at Lee's wedding. It's connected. It's a long story. I'll explain later. Right now, I need that information."

Bryson sat up, wide awake. Tao's tone was all business, cold, void of all emotion. It was his way when he worked an investigation, to the point his colleagues had always thought he had no feelings at all. What Bryson knew that they didn't was Tao's coldness was the most dangerous point Tao could reach before entering the final stage of a case. It was the time he needed someone to act as a buffer.

"Tao, I'm sorry," Bryson said. "I really am. I know how much your uncle meant to you. Are you sure you want to pursue this? You need time."

"Can you get what I need or not?" Tao said.

Bryson cursed under his breath. Tao wasn't going to listen. He needed to grieve, but he wouldn't, not until the matter was finished, if then.

"Yeah," Bryson said, "Yeah, no problem. First thing, I'll get what I can and get it to you."

He paused.

"Tao, I know you. I don't like what I hear. Are you okay? I mean, really okay? Is Lee okay? Can I do anything else to help? What can I do?"

He heard the heavy sigh.

"I'm—managing," Tao said. "Lee—Lee is coping. His brothers are here."

Bryson wanted to say something, do something to ease what he knew Tao must be going through.

"Tell me what's going on," he said.

"I'm not sure," Tao said. "It's a long story. I'm just now putting all the pieces together."

He sounded tired. From past experience, Bryson knew he probably wasn't eating or sleeping.

"Get some sleep, Tao," Bryson said. "I know it's hard for you right now, but you have to get some sleep. Think about Monica. She needs you. Lee needs you."

He could almost picture the scowl on Tao's face.

"I'll try."

It was short, curt, and Bryson knew Tao didn't mean it.

Unexpectedly Tao said, "It's bad, Bry, and I am tired. I can't believe this has happened. I didn't want it to happen."

"Tao," Bryson said, "you aren't blaming yourself for this?"

There was no answer.

"Hang on, buddy," Bryson said. "You're gonna make it. Whatever's happened, it's not your fault. You're a tough guy, remember?"

"Yeah," Tao said, "tough. That's me. Goodnight, Bry."

He disconnected.

Bryson sat for a long time and thought about the conversation. He knew all the danger signs. He knew what he had to do. No one else would and if Tao wasn't held in check things would be a bigger disaster than they obviously were.

Gently, he shook Emily awake.

"I need to take a trip to Hong Kong," he said. "Tao's in trouble. He needs help from somebody who knows how to give it to him."

Emily smiled sleepily at him.

"I know," she said. "I was listening. Take him my love, too."

He took her in his arms and kissed her. He placed his hand on the bulge in her tummy and felt the baby kick. He kissed her again.

"Be careful," she whispered.

With the attack and deaths of Kai Chi and Ki, Tao had no choice but to tell the police the whole story behind the hijacking. The Superintendent wasn't happy that the vital information had been kept from the authorities. He wanted to talk to Lee, but Tao refused even after being threatened with obstructing justice. Out of respect for Lee's grief and family, the Superintendent capitulated, but told Tao he would see Lee after Kai Chi's funera and they would both have a lot of explaining to do.

The information Keung had asked for finally arrived and he gave it and paperwork from the government agency where he worked to the authorities. An all points bulletin was issued for Kim and Taibo to be detained for questioning. Since Tao and Lee's rescue, there had been no word or sight of either of them.

Lee sat in the office at Kai Chi's desk. It was getting dark, but he didn't bother to turn on the lamp. It was quiet and he closed his eyes to let his other senses pick up the parts of his father that lingered in the room.

He'd retreated to that sanctuary wanting to be close to his father and away from everyone else. The wasted years when he and Kai Chi had been at odds weighed heavily on his mind. Sitting in the dark room, he was able to release the grief and anger and regret where no one else could see. He could hear his father's voice, his laughter, and smell the smoke from the cigars Kai Chi liked to smoke. Returning to Hong Kong wasn't supposed to have gone like this. They were all suppose to have lived happily ever after as a family.

He rubbed his arm. It hurt where the bandage covered where the bullet had grazed him.

The wedding party had been escorted by the Coast Guard back to Hong Kong where they were met by ambulances waiting to take the bodies of Kai Chi and Ki away, and the wounded, including Lee, to the hospital. He wanted to stay with Meng, but she insisted that he go and have his arm tended. She sent his older brother, Kai Po, with him. It had taken all of Kai Po's arguing and patience to keep him in Emergency long enough to get the injury treated.

It wasn't until he and Kai Po returned to home, that he discovered no one had seen Tao after they'd reached Hong Kong. He wanted to find him, but was argued out of it, and agreed to stay only after his cousins promised to find out where Tao had gone and see that he was alright.

He went to see about Meng. She was in her room and had been given a sedative. One of her sisters sat with her and advised him to get some rest.

He found Sophie in their suite. She'd been given a sleeping pill by one of his aunts. Her wedding gown lay discarded on the floor. He picked it up. There was blood down the front of it. Grief tore through him, grief for his wife. Their wedding would never be a day they could remember with happiness, only sorrow.

He took off his tux and threw it on the floor next to the gown. Though it was dark, he knew it, too, was covered in his father's blood.

One of his aunts came with a tray of broth and a pill for him. She stood over him until he took the pill and drank the broth, then he lay down next to Sophie and held her until he fell asleep.

In the three days since, he stayed in the office while his brothers, uncles, and aunts tended to the funeral arrangements. He felt guilty about not helping, but couldn't bring himself to leave his father's sanctuary. His brothers had come and sat with him, none of them saying anything. He knew they were hurting as much as he was, but they didn't know what he did and he couldn't share it with them. This was his private struggle.

Sophie came into the office at intervals to be with him. She didn't know what to say or do to help him through his grief. She felt it, too. She'd loved Kai Chi for the way he'd accepted her immediately as one of the family. He and Meng had taken her as their daughter without any reservations. It hurt her to see Meng and Lee in so much pain. Privately, she burned her wedding dress and his tux. She knew part of what he felt was guilt about their wedding. What happened wasn't his fault and when she thought he was ready, she would talk to him about that. For now, it was his grief over his father that mattered most.

Meng remained secluded in her room. The shock of losing Kai Chi had abated and all that was left was the terrible grief and loneliness. She stood and stared into the gardens remembering the years they'd spent together. She'd married him before he'd made his fortune. They'd lived in a small fishing hut their first 10 years, then had moved into a two bedroom house until just after Lee was born. Kai Chi's business was prospering and before Lee was 10, they had moved into a bigger house, shared with Kong, Tia, and Tao. In two years Kai Chi gave that house to Kong and Tia, then moved her and their sons into the house on the Peak. He'd worked hard and beeen wise with his money, and had failed in only one area…his inability to stand up to Kim.

She turned from the window and went to her desk. On it sat photos of her and Kai Chi on their wedding day. They looked so young and happy, ready to face whatever life threw at them. There were photos of her oldest sons and their new wives. All of them would remember their wedding days with joy. Lee and Sophie would never have that. The happiest day of their lives would forever be marred by the death of Kai Chi and Ki.

Meng picked her wedding picture up and looked into Kai Chi's eyes.

"I promise you," she said, "Kim will pay for this."

She replaced the photo on her desk, straightened her small frame and squared her shoulders. Her head lifted and she stared at her reflection in the mirror.

"The pain won't leave until you stand strong," she said. "Think of your children."

The funerals were private. Lee's older brothers, including the third who hadn't been able to attend the wedding, stood with him and Meng.

As she stood through the funeral, however, she shed no tears. Anger and bitterness against the man who had betrayed them all was her strength. She held Lee and Sophie's hands anchoring herself to them. Behind her Monica and Tao were a strong presence. These were her children. She was the head of the house now. She had her family to think about. There was nothing more she could do for Kai Chi except mourn him.

Later at the house, feeling closed in by the family and acquaintances who had come after the funeral, she slipped into the garden to be by herself for a while and was surprised to find Tao alone on the small bridge watching the gold fish. In his black slacks and shirt he looked thin and gaunt to her.

He had made himself scarce, going back with Monica to the apartment the night of the shooting. Monica said it was because he had to be alone. Meng suspected it was because he felt responsible for what had happened. She'd watched him closely, especially that morning at the funeral. He'd stayed close to Monica, but away from the other people. Still he was always where he could watch them coming and going; the Tiger, guarding his territory and his family.

Monica had tried to get him to tell her what he was thinking, what he was feeling, but this time, he'd refused to open up. He was preoccupied and unresponsive. He wouldn't sleep or eat, but paced the apartment at night, or left for hours at a time without explanation. She worried about him, about what had to be going through his mind.

She'd finally come to Meng. She hadn't wanted to disturb Meng's grief, but she didn't know where else to turn. Meng assured her that she would talk to him.

She went to his side and put her arm around his waist. His arm slipped around her shoulders as he pulled her close.

"You're too thin," she said. "You're not eating again."

His gaze remained focused on whatever he was seeing in his mind, but he couldn't suppress the smile.

"You shouldn't be worrying about me," he said.

"I do worry about you," she said. "I know what you're feeling. I know how you are when you're troubled. Tell me. It will help."

"This is my fault," he said. "If I'd not come back…"

She stepped away and turned him to face her. Her hands firmly latched on his arms as she shook him gently.

"Stop that right now,' she said. "This isn't your doing. Kim is an evil man. If you hadn't escaped, he would've killed you with Kong and Tia. Your home is here, with your family. Your Uncle loved you as his son. He wouldn't feel honored by your guilt. He died for you and Lee, for Kong and Tia, for all of us, to save us."

She placed the palm of her hand on his face.

"You're not alone, my nephew—my son. We are family. We will see Kai Chi didn't die in vain."

Tao wrapped his strong arms around his tiny aunt and held her tight. She felt the warmth of the tears he at last let come. She held him, comforted him as when he was a child. He carried his pain far too deep, the same as Kong and Kai Chi had always done. It wasn't healthy.

After a few minutes, he released her and she wiped the tears off of his face.

"Monica is worried about you," she said. "You've shut her out. That's not right. She needs comfort, too."

"I know," he said. "I don't know what to say. I don't know what to do. I just want to…"

His words trailed away.

"Strike out," Meng said. "I know, but we must hold on to each other. The fight is only beginning."

Tao was surprised. Meng no longer looked frail and fragile. Suddenly the years dropped away from her and she stood, determined and ramrod straight. The fire in her eyes had rekindled. The change scared him a little. He was concerned about how long it would last and what would happen if it left her.

"Don't go to the battlefield unless you can stand to fight," he said.

Meng laughed.

"When the battle comes, we stand together and that gives us strength. Take Monica home. Sleep. I'll be fine. So will the others. Right now, your place is with your wife."

He kissed her cheek and attempted another smile before he walked slowly away from her. It saddened her to see the slump of his shoulders. He had strength, but it had been greatly taxed over the past year. He survived on anger at the moment. She understood. At the moment, that same anger was her strength as well. And she wouldn't fail him.

Chapter 30

Lee and Sophie stayed with Meng. Tao and Monica took her advice and went home. They made use of the privacy. Their lovemaking was forceful and driven. Monica matched Tao move for move as they unleashed their emotions. They slept late and were awakened by a knock at the door to the apartment.

Monica moaned and rolled over, unwilling to get up. Tao pulled on his cutoff shorts to answer the door and was surprised to find a UPS deliveryman waiting for him with a package. He signed for it and carried it to the bedroom. The bed was empty and he heard the shower running. He opened the box and was startled to find his disassembled service revolver secured in packing, his holster, his shield, ID wallet, and a packet containing files and a letter.

Tao,

Captain Arama wasn't happy to hear what you've been up to, and knowing your penchant for getting into trouble, per him, you're now on duty and assigned as head detective on the enclosed case. In the file you'll find, along with the information, extradition papers and arrest warrants, plus official permission to conduct an official police investigation in conjunction with the Hong Kong Police Headquarters. Captain Arama has also wisely appointed you a partner. Pick me up at the airport at 10:00 a.m. tomorrow morning. Meet me at the baggage claim area. Don't be late.

Bry.

P.S. Welcome back to the force, buddy.

Tao stared at the letter. It took a second for it to sink in then he glanced at his watch. It was 9:00. The letter was written the day before. He replaced everything in the box and slid it under the bed. He pulled on his jeans, a sweatshirt, and his loafers, grabbed his wallet and keys and went to the bathroom door.

"I have to go pick something up," he shouted through the door. "I'll be right back."

Before Monica could ask questions, he sprinted out of the door and down to the car. He couldn't decide how he felt. He didn't want to be back on duty, but did like the idea of having a valid excuse to conduct an investigation. He'd only meant to use the case file to lead him. He didn't want the police involved. He didn't want to be restrained that way, to have to answer to anyone except himself if something went wrong.

When he reached the airport, he raced another car for the only available parking space, barely squeezing in ahead of the other driver. Without bothering to answer the angry barrage of Chinese, he ran into the airport and down the escalator to the baggage area. He stole a glance at his watch. It was 10 minutes after 10:00. He told himself Customs would take at least 20 minutes. He had plenty of time.

When he slid breathlessly to a stop by the baggage carousel, he found Bryson already there, his bag at his feet, his eye on his watch. He wore a smug grin of satisfaction.

"You're late," he said.

Tao made a face at him too winded to answer.

"How ya doin', buddy?" Bryson asked as he gave Tao a companionable hug.

"Good considering," Tao said between deep breaths, "that I only got your letter an hour ago."

He picked up the bag and led the way through the maze of people in the terminal.

"What's going on?," he asked.

"I'll explain later," Bryson said. "When we're not so public."

Once they were in the car and headed to the apartment, Bryson explalined.

"We're cheduled to meet with a Superintendent Tang at Hong Kong Police Headquarters. I understand he's supposed to be one of the best."

"I don't understand what this is all about," Tao said. "I can't be involved in a case that I have a personal interest in. How'd this happen?"

"Arama caught wind that you'd called," Bryson said. "Then he caught me in the archives. He wanted to know—no, he demanded to know what, in his words "the hell was going on." I tried to make up something, but…"

He shrugged.

"Arama is no dummy, as you well know. He threatened to put me on a year's suspension if I didn't cough up the truth. He would've done it, too."

Tao could imagine Arama's reaction. He'd been on the other end of the Captain's rampages more times than he cared to remember.

"He surprised me though," Bryson said. "Instead of cussing me out—well, he did that anyway—he was on the phone making arrangements. Because you hold a dual citizenship, you're able to work in both jurisdictions. Not only that, but at the time of their deaths, your parents were still citizens of Hong Kong. They hadn't taken their oaths of American citizenship. That gives both countries an interest in solving their murders. It's still classified unsolved."

"But I have a personal involvement," Tao said. "It's a conflict of interest."

"Yeah," Bryson said, "but you're the only eye witness. And someone from the U.S. Navy contacted both Embassies concerning the hijacking of a certain yacht. I expect the full story on that soon."

He looked over at his friend.

"It's going to be hard," he said. "But you've wanted to solve the murder of your parents for years. You said your uncle's death is tied to it. Your expertise will be needed."

Tao wasn't sure he had any expertise that the police didn't. Investigating on his own for his own reasons was one thing. Being involved in an official investigation was something else entirely.

"I guess I better find a room somewhere," Bryson said. "Got any ideas?"

"The apartment," Tao said. "Lee and Sophie are staying with Aunt Meng and there's a third bedroom anyway. Monica won't mind. I don't know how she'll feel about the rest. It could be dangerous. You better know that up front. Uncle Kim is a dangerous man."

"Uncle Kim?" Bryson asked.

Tao had forgotten Bryson didn't know.

"Kim is Ba ba's oldest brother. He killed Ba ba, Mama, Uncle Kai Chi, and my cousin, Ki. Uncle Kai Chi and Ki were killed on Lee and Sophie's wedding day during the reception on our boat."

"Are you sure it was this Uncle?" Bryson asked.

"Uncle Kim has been after me from the minute I got here," Tao said. "He tried to kill me when he hijacked the yacht, threw me overboard, and if Lee hadn't jumped in after me, I wouldn't be talking to you now."

He looked straight ahead, spoke evenly with no emotion.

"I remembered," he said. "I remembered the face of the Mama and Ba ba's killer."

Bryson hadn't anticipated that. After all those years, Tao finally knew what he'd tried so hard to remember. The shock of it had to have knocked him for a loop.

"Your Uncle Kim?"

"Yes," Tao said. "I saw him that day. I locked it all away, but it's slowly been surfacing. His identity was the only thing I couldn't remember. But after the hijacking, it all come back. I saw his face as he shot Mama as clearly as I see you."

"That's what he was afraid of," Bryson said. "That you'd remember."

"It's why he had me thrown overboard and not Lee," Tao said. "He had nothing against Lee. But Lee wouldn't turn on me. Kim gave him that chance."

"Which made him a liability," Bryson said.

"Exactly."

"But why attack the wedding?" Bryson asked.

"I think Uncle Kai Chi and Uncle Keung both suspected the truth," Tao said. "I think they figured it out, but had no proof. I think Kim knew. Lee and I survived, which meant we'd tell what we knew to the authorities. Kim had already killed to hide his secret. He'd do it again."

Bryson blew his breath out between his lips.

"This is more complicated than I thought," he said. "Do the police know this?"

"Not all of it," Tao said. "We didn't tell them who was behind the hijacking until after the weddng incident. We'd planned to keep it between the two of us."

"You and Lee" Bryson said. "What then? What were the two of you planning to do with the information?"

Tao could feel Bryson's gaze boring into him. Bryson read him better than anyone.

"You were planning on going after him," Bryson said.

"I want him," Tao said, his hands gripping the steering wheel so tight his knuckles were white. "I want him to pay for what he's done, what he's put Lee and Aunt Meng through."

They arrived at the apartment and he parked the car.

"Tao," Bryson said, "that's wrong thinking and you know it. This is the reason you became a cop, to solve this case. Everyone who knows you knows that. But be a cop. You're not a vigilante. Let the law bring Kim down. Don't lose what you have now."

He waited and watched. After a minute Tao's hands relaxed their grip on the steering wheel.

"See why I can't be part of this?" Tao asked. "There's too much involved. I don't know if I trust the law enough."

"You do," Bryson said. "You'll do the right thing. I know you, and I'm going to be right behind you to make sure you don't screw up."

"I don't like it, Bryson."

"Let's meet with the Superintendent," Bryson said. "Let's see what he says. If it doesn't feel right, pull yourself off the case."

Without a word, they both left the car and Tao led the way to the apartment where they found a frantic Monica on the phone.

"Never mind," she said, "he's back—and Bryson's with him."

She was clearly surprised to see the visitor. She hung up the phone.

"Where have you been?" she asked.

"I had to pick Bry up at the airport," Tao said.

"That's what you meant," she said, "when you said you had to pick something up."

He nodded and shrugged.

"Very funny," she said.

She turned to greet Bryson with a hug. She wasn't sure why he was there and she wasn't sure she like it. Bryson had told Tao he would send him the information, but he didn't say he would bring it in person.

"What brings you to Hong Kong?" she asked.

"Business," Bryson said.

She gave him and Tao a searching look. She didn't like what she saw. She didn't like what she felt.

"I have a feeling I'm not going to like this," she said.

Chapter 31

Tao had the same feeling. He was right.

"You're not a detective anymore," she said. "Why are you being dragged into this?"

"Because I am still a detective," Tao said. "On leave, until today."

"I have to do this," he said. "It's not just me. It's about Lee and Aunt Meng. It's about Uncle Kai Chi and Ki. Kim is a cold-blooded killer. He won't stop coming after me now he knows I remember."

Monica was close to tears. Too much had happened since their arrival in Hong Kong and she was afraid. Listening to his dreams, seeing it all come to light for him, knowing how dangerous those memories were, she had thought about talking to him about returning to the States. After the funeral, she knew it would be a waste of time. Tao would never leave his family now.

She didn't mind staying in Hong Kong. She loved Meng, Lee, Sophie, and all the aunts and uncles who had welcomed her. But Tao getting involved in police work again wasn't something she'd foreseen or planned on. It was too dangerous. She didn't want to be a police wife.

"You could be killed," she said. "He might be the one who wins."

Tao knew she was right. It could go either way.

"Tao," she said, "don't. I couldn't bear to lose you. It's already been too close too many times."

"We can leave," she said. "We can go back to New York, or even San Francisco, anywhere you want. Just please, don't do this."

"It won't matter where we are," he said. "Uncle Kim will keep coming. He didn't let Ba ba go, not even when Ba ba put a world between them."

Monica turned imploring to Bryson.

"He's right," he said. "Kim is the kind of man who doesn't like leaving loose ends. He's proven that. Tao isn't the only one in danger. You are. Lee

146

and Sophie are. Meng and her sons, Keung and his family—all of them are liabilities. He believes they all know or soon will, otherwise he wouldn't have attacked the wedding."

"Then let the police handle it," Monica said.

Bryson offered her an understanding smile.

"We are. That's why I'm here. That's why Tao has been assigned to active duty."

Monica was crying.

"But Tao doesn't want to be part of this," she said. "I can see it in his eyes. He won't say it. He thinks he has to prove something, but he doesn't. Leave him alone."

Tao took her hands in his.

"I'll be careful," he said. "I'll make every effort not to get hurt again. Please understand, Nikki. I have to do this."

She pulled her hands away.

"No you don't," she said. "This is an obsession. You don't think I know, don't understand, but you're wrong. It's wrong for them to pull you into this. You've too much at stake."

She wiped the tears from her eyes and squared her shoulders.

"And it's wrong of you to agree to it. If you do get hurt or killed, I'll never forgive you."

She went into the bedroom and slammed the door.

Tao leaned his head back and closed his eyes. His head hurt. Her words stung. He felt stupid for thinking he could hide the truth from her. No one knew him better than Monica, even in the short time they'd been together. She was his rock, the one he clung to, the only one with whom he shared the darkness inside of him.

He opened his eyes, sighed, and stood.

"I'll get my things," he said. "Lee's bedroom is over there. The guest room is next to the kitchen. Go settle in."

"Maybe I better not stay here," Bryson said. "I don't think Nikki appreciates my presence right now."

Tao shrugged in a nonchalance he didn't feel.

"You're my partner. You'll stay."

Bryson placed a warning hand on his arm.

"Tao, be careful. Monica's made a change I never expected to see in you. Don't lose her over this. It's not worth it."

Tao didn't meet his gaze. He nodded wordlessly and went into the bedroom without replying.

Monica stood looking out of the window, her arms crossed defensively. He went to her and put his arms around her. He felt her tense at his touch.

"Love me," he whispered.

"I do love you," she said. "That's why I don't want you to do this."

"I know," he said.

She turned and buried her face against his chest.

"Tao, please don't go," she begged.

The warmth of her tears soaked through his shirt. He held her close and kissed the top of her head. After several minutes, she backed away and wiped her eyes. He kissed her nose. He loved her so much. If only she knew how much she would understand. He had to protect her, to protect all of them.

She placed her hand on his cheek.

"I know how much you're grieving," she said. "You're hiding it, protecting yourself. Kai Chi was a father to you even after all these years. You have to grieve, Tao. Don't hold on to this."

He couldn't answer. He looked down. Her hand felt warm against his skin. He kissed her fingers.

"This isn't what I wanted," he said. "It's not why I asked for the file. I want to prove that Kim is the killer. The police can't do it."

"Neither can you," she said.

"Yes I can," he said. "I'm going to. I have to. I just didn't want to do it this way."

"Take yourself off the case," she said.

"I can't do that now," he said. "Arama knew what I was up to and he's made sure I'm on the case so the police can keep an eye on me."

"He's trying to keep you out of trouble," she said.

"Yeah," Tao said. "Whether I'm on duty or on my own, their going to be watching every move I make. I might as well do it with a badge."

Monica sighed in resignation. It made sense in a way.

"What time tomorrow?" she asked.

"Early," he said. "We're supposed to meet with the Superintendent. I'm a Hong Kong cop now."

He tried to smile, but it didn't quite make it to the surface.

"Be careful," Monica said. "If anything happens to you…"

"It won't," he said, and meant it.

Chapter 32

Bryson and Tao arrived at Superintendent Tang's office at 9:00 the next morning. The Superintendent, a slender man with dark hair, a boyish face, and round glasses, greeted them formally. His carriage was aristocratic and his tone no-nonsense.

"I want you two to know," he said, "I don't like what I've heard about you from your superiors in San Francisco. I understand that you, Tao Chi, are somewhat of a—what's the word—maverick? That being so, I caution you against any cowboy heroics here."

Bryson forced his grin behind a sober expression as he glanced at Tao. It wasn't wise to approach the Tiger in that manner.

"How much do you know about Wong Kim Fong's business?" Superintendent Tang asked.

"Nothing," Tao said. "I suspect smuggling of some kind."

"Close, very close," Tang said. "Smuggling, in particular weapons, military secrets, nuclear plans, defectors from Russia to China, and then to America or Australia. He has worked in close contact with Iran, Iraq, Afghanistan, and North Korea."

Tao sat straight in his chair.

"Before Ba ba left for the States?" he asked.

"Before then," Tang said. "Wong Kim has been associated with such activities since the early 1960's.

"Viet Nam," Tao said.

"Yes," Tang said. "We have long suspected that your father knew something of vital importance and Wong Kim didn't want to take the chance he might tell what he knew. He followed your father to America and assassinated him."

"Why Mama?" Tao asked.

"To leave no witnesses," Tang said. "You and your mother were liabilities. You had to be eliminated to prevent his identity from being known."

"How did you know all of this?" Tao asked.

"We have been in contact with the authorities in San Francisco for some months now," Tang said. "Your Uncle Keung initiated an investigation soon after hearing of the deaths of your parents. A great deal has been discovered during that time. I believe he also has many contacts within the government."

"If you knew all of this," Tao said. "Why haven't you done something?"

"We knew nothing," Superintendent Tang said. "We suspected. It wasn't until your Uncle came to us that what we suspected was indeed fact. We didn't know for certain Wong Kim was behind the attack on your cousin's wedding reception. We're still not certain. Without proof, there's little we can do."

Tao started to say something, but Tang held up his hand.

"Think," he said. "Your Uncle Kim was not there. All of the men on the boats and in the helicopter were killed. Can you say for certain they were your Uncle's men?"

Tao had to admit he couldn't. It all happened so fast, there was no way of knowing. But he had no doubts, nor did anyone else in the family. No one else had any reason.

"So," Tang said, "it's up to the two of you to produce the proof. You'll be in charge of the investigation, both of you. This is an experiment between our police force and that of San Francisco. It's sanctioned by both of our governments, since both have associations with the matter. There is much more than the deaths of your parents involved. I don't approve, but I try to keep an open mind."

Bryson glanced again at Tao. He was angry and it showed.

"You'll have a team to work with you," Tang said. "I expect you to work with that team. Is that understood?"

Neither man said anything. Tang took that as their acquiesence.

"Good," he said. "Sergeant Chan will escort you to your team. They have files and information for you to go over and they will fill you in on what we know so far. Good luck, gentlemen."

They stood. The door opened and a young man about Tao's age and build came in. He snapped to attention, then stood for his orders.

151

"Sergeant, escort these two men to the briefing room," Tang said.

He turned again to Tao.

"I would turn you over to Sergeant Chan, but I need him elsewhere. He's one of my best detectives."

The Sergeant lowered his eyes at the praise. He held the door open for them and followed them out. Once in the hall, he blew his breath out in a huff and shook his head.

"I wish he wouldn't do that," he said. "It's embarrassing."

"Be glad he compliments you," Bryson said. "Believe me, our boss could take a few pointers."

The fact that Bryson answered him in Cantonese pleased the Sergeant.

"You understand?" he asked Bryson.

"Our precinct is Chinatown, San Francisco," Bryson said. "It comes in handy."

Sergeant Chan looked at the silent Tao. Tao returned the look without turning his head. He raised his eyebrows and Sergeant Chan laughed. Deep dimples creased his cheeks.

They reached the conference room and the Sergeant introduced them to their group before leaving them.

"Good luck," he said and hurried on his way.

The group leader introduced himself as Niam Kwon and briefed them on what information the team had. It wasn't much more than the Superintendent had already told them. The most important fact was that the team did know where Kim's headquarters were located. Tao was glad because it saved him time trying to dig his Uncle out.

"Surveillance is the best beginning," Niam said.

"Do we have any idea where he is at this moment?" Tao asked. "He's not been seen since…"

"Wong Kim has been right here in Hong Kong," Niam said. "We've had him under surveillance for some time. He's been at his estate. There have been a good many of meetings lately with others there."

"What others?" Tao asked.

"That we don't know," Niam said.

"He's been hiding out at his estate since he hijacked Tao and Lee?" Bryson asked.

"Not hiding," Niam said. "Planning. We have word that he's getting ready a shipment destined for Iraq. We don't know what's in that shipment, but we do know those who will receive it aren't allies."

"When's this shipment leaving?" Tao asked.

"It's set for the day after tomorrow. We're to watch his headquarters, which are at his main warehouse. When he readys the shipment, we're to alert our headquarters and the Coast Guard."

"You're right," Tao said. "That's the best thing. We'll watch and see if we can find out what he's moving. Maybe we'll find something useful. In any event, we'll know when he's ready to leave."

He sounded perfectly reasonable, in command, listening to his men. Bryson stared at him. It wasn't normal behavior. Tao was obviously angry that so much information had been kept from him, especially that Kim had been under his nose all the time. The police had deliberately kept the family out of the loop and clearly considered the murders of secondary importance.

On Niam's order, the team packed their gear and drove to the site where they would conduct their surveillance of the warehouse. Tao and Bryson followed them in Tao's car.

"You going to tell me what you're up to?" Bryson asked.

Tao kept his eyes forward and his mouth tightly clamped.

"C'mon, Tiger. I know you better than that," Bryson said. "You have no intention of working with this team. You're using them to get to Kim. What are you up to?"

Tao glanced at him and tightened his fingers around the steering wheel.

"He's been right under our noses," he said. "All this time the police knew. Uncle Keung and Uncle Kai Chi probably knew."

He had to fight back his anger.

"But no one told us. Why didn't they do something?"

"They didn't have absolute proof," Bryson said. "You and Lee kept that to yourself, remember?"

Tao did remember. He was angry at himself. If he and Lee had told the truth about the hijacking, Kai Chi and Ki might still be alive.

He hit the steering wheel with his fist.

"Damn!"

He shook his head.

"I just can't sit and wait," he said. "Not any longer."

"I know," Bryson said. "What are you going to do?"

"I'm going for a closer look," Tao said. "Keep the team from noticing?"

Bryson didn't like it.

"Tao, it's too risky. You take too many chances. It's caught you in the back more than once. And we're walking on a thin wire as it is."

"I don't care about what he's moving," Tao said. "I want him because of Mama, Ba ba, and Uncle Kai Chi."

"I know that," Bryson said. "But you can't do this alone. We'll get him and that'll be the end of it. It doesn't matter why he goes to jail as long as we get him off the streets."

When Tao didn't answer, he went on.

"Okay. But reconnaissance only. You'll have one hour. If you find out what Kim's moving, the better for us, but if you're not back by then, I'm coming after you with the entire force."

The team's van had pulled up in back of an old warehouse and the members of the team were unloading. Tao pulled in behind them. Before he and Bryson left the car, they shook hands. Bryson watched to make sure no one noticed when Tao slipped away.

Tao worked his way to the alley and eased along the wall to the street.

He hunched down and peered around the edge of the building. Between him and his uncle's headquarters, the street was empty and silent.

A wave of déjà vu swept over him. Sweat broke out and he shivered and closed his eyes. The vision came immediately of another silent empty street, another alley, another building. His shoulder and chest ached. The back of his head throbbed. His hands shook. He took several deep breaths. They were only memories.

He saw the car pull up and ducked down. Kim, Taibo, and two of Kim's bodyguards climbed out and walked towards the warehouse. Tao felt rage tightening in his chest.

He remembered Palau's visit to Kai Chi's house and wondered if his aunt had really not known where Kim was or if she'd been in on his plans. He knew too little about Kim and his family. He didn't care what Kim was up to. That was a matter for the police. All that mattered to him was the eight left dead by Kim's attacks. He held no doubts that Kim had sent the commandos. He didn't care what Tang thought.

"Do you see them, buddy?" Bryson's voice whispered in his ear.

He jumped. He'd forgotten about the wire he and Bryson rigged earlier that morning before meeting with Superintendent Tang.

"Yes," he hissed. "That's Kim and Taibo in front."

"Be careful, Tao," Bryson said. "I mean it."

"Don't worry," Tao said. "Just keep me in sight."

He waited until the men were inside then slipped across the street to the side of the warehouse. Cautiously he made his way along the building to the ladder leading to the roof. He climbed it and eased over the edge of the roof to the ventilation chimney. Through the wire he heard someone on the team exclaim, "what the hell—" as whoever it was noticed where he was. He heard Bryson warn them to remain at their posts and the protests of Niam on the break of protocol and orders.

Leaning close to the chimney, Tao listened to the voices below in what he hoped was Kim's office. He only heard half of it. Some of the voices were too faint.

"Tao, watch out!" Bryson shouted through his earpiece.

Tao whirled just in time to avoid Taibo's kick.

Chapter 33

Lee returned to the apartment to check on Tao and Monica. It was hard to think since Kai Chi's death. Everything ran together in a constant blur of voices and faces and his only solace was being alone with Sophie holding him through his bouts of guilt. He and Kai Chi had spent too many years in silence. Returning home, finding his father held no grudges meant more to him than he could have asked. It had been too brief. There was much more left for them. Kim had stolen it away.

Lee understood Tao more than ever because now they shared the pain of loss. He'd spent hours being comforted by Sophie, Meng, and even his brothers, but Tao had only Monica.

Meng had asked him to check on Tao. That made him realize that he'd been so wrapped up in his own grief that he'd forgotten about Tao.

He arrived at the apartment and noticed the silence as soon as he entered the door. He checked Tao's room and his room, then noticed the door to the third room was open. When he went in he saw the suitcase on the bed.

"Bryson's here,' Monica said behind him.

He turned.

"Where were you?" he asked.

"In the bathroom," she said.

He noticed her face was pale, her eyes puffy and red from crying.

"Bryson?" he asked. "What's he doing in Hong Kong?"

"Trying to get them both killed," she said. "I told you Tao called him. He showed up yesterday with papers putting Tao back on duty."

"He can't be," Lee said. "They can't do that."

"Tao and Bryson have been assigned to the Hong Kong police," Monica said.

"I don't understand," Lee said. "What for?"

"Kai Chi's murder," she said. "Kai Chi's murder is connected to the death of Tao's parents."

She handed him the file she'd found under the bed. He accepted it beginning to understand. He remembered Kim's admission to him on the yacht.

"Tao's personally involved in both cases," he said. "They can't assign him to them."

Monica sank wearily into a chair and hugged herself.

"Bryson said it's because Tao is the only eye witness to both killings."

Lee knew Tao wanted Kim in the worst way. So did he. But if Tao found Kim and Taibo before anyone else, there would be no controlling him.

He started pacing the floor. Meng had been right to be worried. Tao and Monica had been deeply affected by Kai Chi's murder, the same as the rest of the family. They should've stayed at the house among those who cared for them.

Lee knelt on one leg in front of Monica and lifted her chin with his finger so she looked at him.

"When did they leave?" he asked. "Where did they go?"

"About an hour ago," she said, "to meet a Superintendent named Tang at Police Headquarters."

Lee took her gently by the shoulders.

"I want you," he said, "to go now to the house. Let Mama take care of you. Mama and Sophie are worried about you and they need you. Don't—try not to worry about Tao. He's a good cop—the best. He knows what he's doing. He'll be okay."

He knew he was trying to convince himself more than her. He had to make himself believe it. He wasn't sure a badge would keep Tao in check. He didn't know what kind of a cop Tao was. He only knew what he'd been told by Bryson and Emily, and that didn't ease his mind any.

"If Tao finds his uncle," Monica said. "We both know what he'll do. He hates Kim. It won't matter how good he is, he hates him. Kim murdered three people Tao loved most. He won't be able to let it go."

Lee hugged her. She understood too much. He wished Tao had heard her words.

"Don't worry," he said, "I'll find him. I'll keep him from crossing that line, I promise."

Her tears were hot against his shoulder.

"How?"

"I'll find a way," he said.

Tao landed in a crouch, his dark eyes fixed on Taibo's sneering face.

"I've been expecting you, little cousin," Taibo said. "You've taken longer than I expected."

He circled Tao warily. Tao's eyes never left his face.

Tao shoved every emotion deep to let cold nerve take over. This would decide. He had to become the Tiger to survive.

"I told Uncle you would come," Taibo said. "When we heard about your rescue, I knew you would come."

He laughed nastily.

"He didn't believe me. He thought you'd be afraid, that you'd consider it too dangerous to fight after being left to die at sea. But he doesn't know you."

He stopped, his expression dark and dangerous.

"But I know you. All too well, I know you. I made it a point to know you, to know your habits, your ways. I was told that you never give up, that you hold on, stalk, watch, and wait. I saw you slip out of the alley like a ghost."

Tao emptied his mind of everything except Taibo's presence. Taibo may have checked into Tao's background as a detective, but knowing and confronting were two different things. A lot of others had made the same mistake.

His silence played on Taibo's nerves.

"You're not alone are you?" Taibo said. "It doesn't matter. You're too far from any help. You take chances, but this time it's going to cost you."

Taibo took a long blade knife from a sheath on his belt. Tao's expression showed nothing as he eased his stance. Taibo was taking too much for granted.

Taibo charged. Tao waited until the last second, then brought his leg up and slammed it into Taibo's middle. He rolled with the kick in midair, his other leg catching Taibo on the side of the head. Taibo went down, rolled, and sprang to his feet. With the back of his hand, he wiped the blood from his mouth.

"First blood," he said.

Tao landed agily on his feet ready for another attack. He met Taibo's second onslaught with flying fists. Taibo tried to sweep in under him, but couldn't bypass the raining blows of his more experienced cousin.

The knife swept through the air, but Tao avoided it. In his ear he could hear Bryson, witnessing the battle from the roof of the other building, shouting orders and yelling for backup.

The battle raged over the roof. Each man attempted to drive the other to the lip of the building and over the side. Tao was the expert. Taibo, well-trained though he was, failed to find a breach. His knife slashed through the air and caught the fabric of Tao's shirtfront and sleeve.

Tao rushed him and drove him against the air vent. He pinned him and rammed the hand holding the knife against the hard metal surface until Taibo let go. Tao turned and flipped Taibo over his shoulder. He hit the roof hard as Tao kicked the knife out of reach.

The sound of gunshots echoed between the buildings. There was shouting, the sound of running feet, glass breaking and doors crashing open. The door to the roof burst open. Kim's men flooded the roof. Kiam and his team swarmed after them. Sirens were blaring from the streets. Police cars screeched to a halt and more police poured into the building and onto the roof.

"Tao, watch out!" Bryson's voice reached his ears.

Tao dove sideways just in time to avoid the bullet that whistled past.

He scrambled for cover as Kim fired again at Bryson who had reached the roof by way of the fire escape. Bryson ducked then threw himself over, rolled and dove out of the way of the third shot.

Kim's gun kept Bryson and Tao pinned down behind their cover. Tao saw Taibo's knife only a few feet away. Gauging the distance, he waited until Kim fired. Taking a deep breath, Tao launched himself at the knife, grabbed it, rolled to his feet and shouted.

Kim took his shot. In that instant he was visible. Tao barrelled into him. Kim's gun came up but he never fired. Bryson yelled and distracted him.

Kim was bigger, but Tao's rage was his strength. He held Kim on his back and fought to reach his neck with the knife. Kim's hand clamped tight on Tao's wrist to break the hold. As he looked deep into the dark brown eyes of his nephew, he saw nothing would stop him from his own form of justice.

"Kill me and you're the same as I," he hissed.

"Tao!" Bryson shouted.

It broke the spell. Tao's head lifted. Taibo stood two feet from him, a gun leveled at him. An animal growl left Tao's throat. He bared his teeth in a snarl and charged.

Kim scrambled to his feet. The gun fired. On the move, Bryson shoved Tao to one side. It put him between Tao and the bullet that went straight through his shoulder and out of his back. The bullet hit Kim in the heart just as he raised his gun to shoot Tao.

Tao stumbled and before he could regain his balance, Taibo vanished. Tao pushed through the chaos of the fighting and ran to Bryson who lay on his back holding his wound.

"I'm sorry, Bryson," he said, tearing off his shirt and pressing it over the wound. "Why did you do that?"

Bryson laughed weakly.

"That's what friends are for," he said.

He coughed and gritted his teeth against the pain.

"Isn't it?"

Chapter 34

Patrick came to attention when Lee came tearing out of the apartment.

"Tao's gone," Lee said as he scrambled into the car. "The police have gotten him involved in Ba ba's murder."

"He's gone after Kim?" Patrick asked.

Lee nodded, his eyes glued to the road as he sped towards the Police Headquarters.

"I'm not sure how, but Tao's Captain had him and his friend from San Francisco assigned to the investigation. They don't realize what they've done."

Patrick knew. He remembered all too well Tao's fiery temper and determination. He'd already been pushed to his limits. Bringing him into the investigation was a dangerous mistake.

Patrick had sent Tina back to the States after the attack at the wedding. He'd remained for Lee's sake. Lee was strong, but he had loved his father dearly, despite their differences of opinion.

"What are you going to do?" he asked.

"If Tao finds Kim and Taibo before the police," Lee said, "there'll be no going back. I've got to stop him."

Patrick said nothing. He worried about his friend. If Lee lost Tao on top of losing Kai Chi, the devastation might overwhelm him. He'd been courageous and fearless as a fireman, professional and stable as a Captain. Much of that had changed after the fire.

A few minutes later they slid to a stop in front of the police station and were standing in Superintendent Tang's office.

"You don't understand," Lee said. "Tao's a good detective, but right now he's under a lot of strain. He hates hard. He hides inside of himself. That's when he's most dangerous. Our uncle is a killer. I hate him. Tao hates harder than I do. If he finds him, he'll kill him."

"You believe that?" Tang asked. "You believe he hasn't enough restraint and professionalism to do his duty and do it right."

"Under normal circumstances," Lee said. "But these aren't normal.

He remembered Arturo Gravelli whose body was never found. He would never admit to Tao that he suspected Arturo was already dead when the building exploded. He was never sure if Tao wouldn't kill if pushed too far.

"I think you're mistaken," Tang said. "My impression is that he'll do his job. I trust that. I have to believe it."

His phone rang and he answered it. His face drained of color and Lee was on immediate alert. When Tang replaced the receiver he turned uneasily to Lee.

"The warehouse is under siege," Tang said.

"Warehouse?" Patrick asked.

"Wong Kim's headquarters," Tang said. "It was under surveillance—but now—you'd better come with me. We may need your help."

Nothing but silence greeted them at the warehouse when they arrived. Police were leading men in custody to waiting police vehicles. Ambulances waited for the wounded. The area looked like a battlefield.

They found Tao on the roof sitting with his back against the vent. Bryson lay with his head on Tao's lap. Tao's hand firmly pressed a bloody shirt against Bryson's shoulder.

Patrick carefully removed the shirt to look at the injury. Bryson was awake and smiled through his pain as the wound was examined.

"We need to get you to the hospital," Patrick said. "It's not fatal, but your shoulder will be out of commission for a while."

"Good," Bryson said. "It gives me an excuse to be home when the baby comes."

"Due soon?" Patrick asked.

He was glad to see that Bryson was in good spirits despite the pain he was in.

"Yeah," Bryson said. "Emily won't be very happy about this."

Lee examined Tao. Other than bruises and a few minor cuts, he seemed unhurt. He was withdrawn, having done what he came to do. Lee knew he was aware that he would have a lot of questions to answer. He glanced over his shoulder at the shrouded figure lying several feet away.

"Tao didn't kill him," Bryson said. "That bullet was meant for him. That's how this happened. The bullet went through me and hit Kim."

"That means…" Lee said.

"Taibo," Bryson said. "He took off afterward."

Tao's eyes moved to Lee's face. Lee was relieved because he knew that Tao was listening. He brushed Tao's hair out of his face.

"He's shut down," Bryson said. "He does that. It's his defense."

Superintendent Tang came over to them, a grim expression on his face. "Are they alright?" he asked.

Lee was angry. If Tang hadn't brought Tao into this—he hesitated. What would have happened? He couldn't answer that question. He'd vowed in the hospital that he wanted Kim dead as much as Tao.

"No," he said.

Tang called for the paramedics.

"What happened here, Wong?" he asked Tao.

"Ambushed," Tao said, his voice barely above a whisper.

"Leave him alone," Lee said. "You've caused enough damage."

"Wong Kim is dead," Tang said. "I have to know why. This was to be surveillance only. What went wrong? He has the answer to that."

"Find Taibo," Tao said. "He got away."

"I'll find him," Tang said. "You haven't answered my question."

"Find Taibo," Tao said again. "And you'll find your answer."

Chapter 35

The apartment was dark when Tao arrived home. He was exhausted after spending hours first in the emergency room of the hospital then in Superintendent Tang's office explaining what happened at the warehouse. Lee stayed by his side for support against the barrage of questions, and at last Tang seemed satisfied that Tao's action against his uncle hadn't been revenge, only to gather information.

Lee told him that he'd sent Monica to Meng, but when Tao called to let her know he was alright and to make sure she was, he was informed by Sophie that Monica hadn't shown up. He was worried, but he said nothing to Lee other than Monica had changed her mind and decided to stay home. He told Lee that he was going home to be with her and drove to the apartment as fast as he could.

There was empty silence when he entered. Moonlight cast a blue light through the panoramic window. Tao listened, but heard nothing. He felt the tension, knew what it was that pervaded his senses, every corner of the room, the entire apartment.

He crossed to the bedroom. Slowly he pushed opened the door.

He knew what he would find even before he'd called Meng's. He'd wanted to tell Tang to shove his questions, that he had to get home. Now he stood in the doorway of the bedroom knowing that it wasn't finished. There was still more to do.

He closed his eyes, breathed deep, and remembered the night he'd met Monica. Love me forever.

How many times had he whispered those words? His anger was against himself for his inability to let go of the past, to turn away from the self-destructive path. He'd placed her in the middle of the danger and had only himself to blame.

Kim was dead, but Taibo had escaped. Was it worth Monica's life?

The doorbell rang. He went to the door and jerked it open. He'd seen her standing across the street, waiting, watching for him to arrive. He knew she'd been waiting on him because she'd started across to the apartments as soon as he got out of the car.

"What do you want, Ling?"

The tiny woman stood, her simple gray dress and black shoes blending into the shadows of the corridor. Her head lowered, her long black hair a veil around her face, she refused to meet his gaze. She held an envelope out to him.

"This is for you," Ling said, her voice filled with fear.

He was unable to see her clearly in the shadows. He reached his hand to gently lift her face where he could see it. Dark ugly bruises marred her pretty features.

"Come inside," he said.

Meekly she obeyed.

"Did Taibo do this to you?" he asked.

She said nothing.

"Ling," Tao said, "tell me."

She lifted her gaze and he saw what he expected to see. He couldn't be angry with her. Her misery was also his fault.

"My father owed much money to Wong Kim," she said. "He thought you would give money if I said I had your child."

She was crying, wiping the tears with the back of her hand. Tao handed her a kleenex.

"I never wanted you to suffer," she said. "Father refused to tell you we were no longer married. I begged him, but he was angry because you didn't stay."

"I'm sorry, Ling," Tao said.

"Why?"

"For—what I did," he said. "I should never have asked you father…"

She placed her fingers against his lips.

"No," she said. "You don't understand. He told me to take you to the hills that night. He wanted you to want me. Wong Kim has had my father in his power for years," she said. "Ba ba didn't welcome you because you were

Kong's friend. He wanted you because it would mean he would be part of Kim's family."

She sat down in a chair and shook her head.

"I didn't want to marry you. He told me what he was doing. I hoped that I wouldn't mean anything to you, that you would leave. I didn't want to hurt you. You'd already been hurt so much, but I knew of no other way to make you go. If I'd known you still thought—I would've sent a letter. I didn't know Ba ba hadn't told you."

She took time to blow her nose and try to wipe away the smeared mascara.

"It was father-in-law's idea about the little boy," she said. "I didn't want to do it. My husband argued with him about it, told him it was wrong, but he is as ruthless as Wong Kim. He told us my husband's job depended on my cooperation. My husband is his only son, but he said he would disown him and leave us destitute if I refused."

She offered Tao a sad smile.

"I love my husband," she said. "He's always been good to me, but his father and Ba ba are partners. And they're both deeply in debt to Wong Kim."

"How much?" Tao asked.

"I don't know. But it's a lot. To keep his business, Ba ba had to do what Wong Kim told him. If you didn't pay the money, Wong Kim would take everything and destroy Ba ba. That would destroy my husband's father and my husband."

Tao felt his chest tighten. He had carried his resentment towards Ling for her inability to love him, but he'd been wrong.

"How long has your father owed Kim money?" he asked.

"As long as I can remember," she said.

"Kim is dead," Tao said.

She nodded and placed the letter in his hand.

"But Taibo lives," she said. "And he has never been far from Wong Kim's shadow."

Tao glanced at the envelope.

"He sent you?"

She nodded again.

"He'll kill my husband if I don't deliver this letter. He's already killed Ba ba."

"What?" Tao wasn't prepared for that.

"Ba ba is dead," she said. "I don't care anymore because of the things he made me do. But, my husband—please Tao, I know you hate me, but…"

He placed his fingers on her cheek and gently kissed her forehead.

"No, I don't hate you," he said. "I'm not sure I ever did. I just didn't understand. Now I do. You did it for your father and held your silence for 10 years because you loved him. You're a good daughter."

"I held my silence because I honored you," she said. "I'm a fool because I obeyed my father."

For the first time, Tao felt compassion as he took her in his arms and held her.

"I must go," she said.

"Wait." He opened the envelope.

A necklace dropped into his hand, a silver dragon entwined around a jade pendent. He read the note.

"Please, Tao," Ling said. "I must go."

You killed Kim. Can you find your precious wife before she joins him?

Taibo

He pulled his gun from his waistband holster and checked the chambers. Ling cringed.

"Take me to him," he said.

She backed away, terrified.

"I can't. I don't know where he is. He gave me the letter at our home and sent me to you."

"Then we'll start there," he said.

"But he'll kill them," she said.

He led her out of the apartment and down the stairs to the street.

"He won't know I'm there," he said. "I promise."

He started to unlock the car door when he heard the squeal of tires and the roar of an engine. A black car flew towards them, its light momentarily blinding him.

"No!" Ling screamed.

167

She ran forward and shoved him out of its path. It struck her hard and threw her over the hood into the street.

Tao pulled his gun and was aiming at the car when Ling pushed him. He landed on his side and scrambled up almost in one motion, but not soon enough to avoid hearing the terrible impact or seeing Ling's broken body sail through the air. He ran to her and eased her onto her back. Blood trickled from her mouth and nose.

"*Dui m jue,*" she gasped between ragged breaths. "*Ngoh foon sue.* Forgive me."

"*Ngoh hai jo.* I do," he whispered.

He rocked her in his arms, his tears falling on her face as her gaze faded non-seeing into death. She'd never loved him, but had been his first love. She'd been his wife though he'd never shared his life with her. She'd done everything her father had ordered, but had given her life for his. He wished it'd been him. It was too much. The day he was shot, he'd wished for death and it'd come, but never for him.

Sirens cut through the night. Voices spoke to him. People touched him, but reality became the flame of burning vengeance. As Ling was gently lifted from his arms and he was helped to his feet, his only thoughts were of Taibo. Monica would not become another victim. Taibo would pay for entering the domain of the tiger.

Chapter 36

Superintendent Tang stormed into his office and threw the file on his desk. He should have held Wong Tao Chi. He should have made him tell him everything, especially about his connection to the woman Hualin Lei Ling killed outside of the Wong apartment. Her death put a new light on the case.

After the officers responded to the hit and run accident, they alerted their superiors and detectives were sent to the scene. There was no one at the apartment and the last anyone had seen of Tao Wong, he'd been at the accident, then had disappeared.

Tang sent officers to the Hualin home and Wong home to inform the families of Ling's death and Tao's disappearance.

At the Hualin home, Lei Ling's husband and father-in-law were found in Hualin's office shot through the back of the head. It was Tao's good fortune that at the time of their deaths, according to the medical examiner, he was being questioned in Tang's office.

The coroner discovered the note clasp in Lei Ling's hand, raising more questions about what she'd been doing at Tao Wong's home.

A few hours after the detectives paid their visit to Meng, Lee arrived at the police headquarters accompanied by Patrick. He read the note and felt responsible because he'd left Monica to go to Meng's alone. He should have taken her there himself before going to the warehouse. He'd known there was a possibility that she might be in danger.

He informed Tang that Tao and Taibo had been at each other's throats from the moment Tao had set foot in Hong Kong. There had seemed to be no reason for Taibo's persecution until the day Kim took control of the yacht. Kim had as much as told Lee that he was responsible for the deaths of his brother and sister-in-law. He was responsible for the deaths of Kai Chi and his nephew, Ki, as well as for the near drowning of Lee and Tao.

169

Tang was of a mind to put Lee in jail for not telling him all of the facts concerning the hijacking. If he'd had that information, he could have moved sooner on Kim Wong and the fiasco at the warehouse might have been avoided. He immediately put out an all points bulletin for Wong Tao Chi to be detained for questioning. In reality, he wanted to get hold of the hotheaded young man before he did something he would regret later.

No one had any idea where Tao was. He was on the prowl, and according to Captain Arama, that was when he was the most lethal. There was no doubt in Tang's mind that Taibo was the one who'd killed Ling, her father, father-in-law, and husband. Once he'd received the file on Tao's marriage to Lei Ling and the subsequent results of that ill-fated affair, everything concerning the two of them fell into place. But he couldn't figure out what their connection was with Kim Wong other than Tao.

A knock on the door of his office interrupted his thoughts.

"Come!"

The door opened and Sergeant Chan entered, snapped to attention with a crisp salute, and handed him another file.

"We've discovered Lei Ling's father was deeply indebted to Wong Kim," the Sergeant said. "Several million American dollars, and for many years."

Tang glanced through the file.

"His wife is deceased," Chan said. "Lei Ling was an only child. Witnesses to the marriage of Lei Ling and Tao say the whole thing was arranged by her father. He wanted Tao to be part of his family so he would be linked to Wong Kim."

"Tao didn't stay in China," Lee said. "Lei Ling refused to go with him when he returned to the States. Only recently was he told their marriage was annulled a long time ago."

"Then this has to be the link," Tang said. "If she married him in obedience to her father, what else might she have done?"

"She called Tao," Lee said, "and told him she had his child. There never was a child, only a picture. Ling's husband told us later she'd been put up to it."

Superintendent Tang sat down behind his desk and leaned forward on his elbows.

"If Lei Ling's father was as in debt to Kim as much as it appears, that could have been a ploy to coerce money from Tao. Wong Kai Chi was a wealthy man and he accepted Tao as a son. It makes sense. I would be willing to bet she delivered the note to draw him out."

"You think she was a lure?" Lee said. "That the driver meant to kill Tao?"

"Or both of them," Tang said, "but he missed Tao."

"And now Tao Wong is hunting the killer," Chan said.

"Who's taken Monica as bait," Lee said.

"Find the last known address on Taibo Wong," Tang said to Chan. "Get out there and see what you can find."

"Already done," Chan said. "Taibo Wong left Hong Kong late last night. I've checked the airlines. There is no Taibo Wong on any flights listings, but there is someone by the name of Kim Lee Huanlin who fits his description and was traveling with an American woman who fits the description of Monica Wong."

Superintendent Tang was on his feet and reaching for his hat. Lee and Patrick stood with him.

"Where was the plane headed?" Tang asked as he led them out of the office.

Sergeant Chan, Lee, and Patrick hurried to keep up with him.

"San Francisco," Chan said.

Lee and Patrick left the police headquarters and went to the hospital to see Bryson and fill him in on what was going on.

Bryson was as worried as they were. Taibo had crossed the line when he kidnapped Monica. Tao would never let go until he found and took down his cousin. In doing so, he would himself become a killer.

Lee, Patrick, and he went over every detail about where Taibo might go, what he would do, or if he would hurt Monica.

"Would he dare hurt her?" Patrick asked. "Just how dangerous is Tao at this moment?"

"Extremely," Bryson said. "Finding Taibo and freeing Monica alive is all he'll care about. The possibility of his own death won't concern him. He'll make sure Taibo goes down first."

Using all his resources in San Francisco, Bryson did some quick phoning.

It took most of the afternoon and evening to find out when Taibo had left Hong Kong and what flight he'd been on to the States. There was just enough time for Lee and Patrick to get the last flight to San Francisco. Lee promised Bryson to let Emily know he was okay and would soon be home. He also promised Bryson he would find Tao and stop him before it was too late, the same promise he'd made to Monica—and he'd failed.

From the airport, he phoned Sophie and explained to her what was happening. He thought about asking her not to tell Meng, but decided that would be a waste of time. Meng would be able to tell that Sophie was keeping something from her.

Tao didn't bother trying to hide his identity as he took the taxi to the airport. He knew the police would be looking for him, but they weren't yet.

He'd gone to Ling's home and found the bodies of her father-in-law and husband. He understood that the car hadn't been meant just for him. Ling was meant to die as well.

Too many people had died on his account. It had to stop. He had to stop it. As he sat on the plane and stared into the night, he thought about Monica, about how much he loved her. If she decided to leave him after this, he wouldn't stop her, but he would never allow anything to happen to her. He couldn't live without her, but would willingly give his life for her. If something did happen to him, at least then the past would be laid to rest, buried with him, and Monica could go on, safe, and find someone to love and make her happy.

He'd been having flashbacks to the last few months on the force. It was happening all over again, the oppressive fatigue, the struggle to face the pain and the violence. He'd wanted it to stop then and he wanted it to stop now.

Taibo shoved Monica into the dark apartment. Her hands were tied behind her back. Her eyes were blindfolded, and unable to catch her balance, she stumbled and fell hard.

Taibo jerked her to her feet and pulled the blindfold off her eyes. He leered at her and the look made her sick. He hadn't touched her, but she didn't trust that to last. He was a murderer and he hated Tao. He would do the worst to taunt and torment his cousin.

She'd heard the front door of her apartment open and thought it was Tao

172

returning from police headquarters. When she went into the livingroom to ask him how it went, Taibo had grabbed her from behind the bedroom door and held a cloth over her nose. She'd blacked out and had awakened next to him on the plane already airborne. He informed her he'd told the attendants that she was his alcoholic wife, drunk as usual. He warned her not to draw attention to herself or try to get away if she wanted to live. She hadn't doubted him. She knew she was a lure for Tao and the thought terrified her. But what she didn't understand was why they were leaving Hong Kong.

"Oh, don't worry, cousin," Taibo said, as he pushed her onto the bed. "I'm not going to hurt you. Not yet."

He squatted in front of her and took her chin in his fingers. It hurt and brought tears to her eyes.

"Don't worry about dear Tao, either," he said. "He'll come. I left a broad trail. He'll have no trouble following."

He straightened and opened a soft leather case lying on the bed. It had been waiting for him in an airport locker after they had cleared Customs. He smiled as he lifted the parts of the rifle and fitted them together.

"And when he does," he said, more to himself than to her, "we'll end this little game once and for all."

Chapter 37

Captain Arama knew it was going to be bad. Superintendent Tang had filled him in on everything. Bryson Royo had been shot. Emily Royo was demanding explanations. The killer was on his way to San Francisco and Tao was most assuredly right behind him.

That was the part that worried Captain Arama the most. The young detective had erupted on other cases, but his badge had always restrained him from going too far. Arama didn't know if Tao wearing a badge would help this time. It was only temporary and this case was personal. If anything happened, it would be Arama's fault. When he found out what Bryson was doing for Tao and why, he thought putting Tao on the case would keep him in line. He thought Bryson would help curb the impulsiveness. He'd been wrong and if things went wrong, his own badge would be on the line along with Tao's.

He put out the order that Tao Wong be picked up the moment his plane landed. Superintendent Tang had faxed him a photograph of Taibo and Monica Wong. But by the time he received the information, that flight had come and gone. Tao's flight was just landing.

Arama looked at his watch. His phone rang. He snatched it up, listened, then slammed it down in anger. He'd expected it. Tao had eluded them. He'd spotted the surveillance team long before they saw him.

Arama grabbed the phone.

"Linden," he said, "find out if any cabs outside the airport picked up a fare matching the description of any one of the Wongs...I know there are a lot of cabs. Just do it!"

He dropped into his chair and tiredly ran his hand through his hair. He shouldn't have sent Bryson with the file. If he hadn't, it wouldn't have altered the situation, but Bryson would be safe at home with his wife, not in a Hong Kong hospital.

The phone rang again. Arama grabbed it.

"We have a match," Lindon reported. "Taibo Wong and Tao's wife were taken to an apartment building in Chinatown. I've got the address."

When he gave it, Arama sat up, his gut clenching.

"My god!" He rubbed his hand over his face.

"Sir?"

"Get going!" Arama bellowed. "Find that building before Tao gets there. If he arrives or is there, arrest him. Do not—I repeat—do not let him near Taibo or that apartment."

"Yessir," Linden said and rang off.

Arama leaned into his chair and closed his eyes. It was the worst news. Taibo was leading Tao to the place where it all began. It might very well be a fatal mistake for both of them.

Taibo looked from behind the curtain of the window facing the street. He wasn't smile now. His face was dark, a predator hiding in the shadows, waiting.

Monica sat on the bed, her ankles and arms bound, a gag over her mouth. Her throat was raw and dry, her eyes swollen from crying.

Over her initial fright, she'd taken a good look at the apartment. It was small and had been deserted for sometime, but there was still the furniture, the bed, table and chairs, a stove and a refrigerator in the room where she was. There was a hall that she assumed led to another bedroom and a bathroom. There were cobwebs and dust and at first she couldn't figure out why Taibo had brought her there, then she made the connection. Tao would come, even if it meant facing that place, a place that to him meant death.

She closed her eyes and tried to ease the cramp in her shoulders. They had been there a full day. She was thirsty and sick to her stomach, but she kept her silence. She didn't dare antagonize Taibo who paced back and forth in front of the window, his eyes never leaving the street below.

Suddenly a handful of her hair was wrapped around his fingers and her head was jerked back. She opened her eyes and did her best not to show fear.

"What are you sniveling for?" Taibo said. "For Tao? Is that it?"

He let go of her hair with a snap of his wrist.

"He's not worth your tears," he said as he leaned close to her.

175

She felt his hot breath against her skin and was repulsed. His eyes glittered with savage amusement.

"I'm more of a man than he'll ever be," he said. "Let me show you."

She stiffened as he unbuttoned several buttons on her blouse. One hand slid along her thigh to reach her hip and trace the outline of her underwear. Cold shivers ran through her as she tried not to cringe. A moment later, he stood, his laugh ugly, taunting.

"No," he said, "not yet. Not until Tao is here, just before I kill him. I'll let him witness a real man in action."

He returned to the window.

She swallowed her fear and felt a hatred she'd never experienced in her life. She thought of what Tao had witnessed moments before his mother was murdered. Taibo meant for him to go through it again.

Tao studied the curtain on the second floor of the building across the street from the alley where he waited.

Taibo had lead him to this place to make him suffer, maybe run from the fear. But Tao wasn't afraid. He'd faced those demons a long time ago, come to this neighborhood and stood in the same place watching the little market and the apartment above it. They had been empty for years. Kong's lawyer had placed most of Kong and Tia's belongings in storage until Tao turned 17. Some of the furniture remained, but nothing of value. On Tao's 17th birthday, the lawyer had contacted him concerning his parents' wish that, should anything happen to them, their ashes be returned to their family shrine in China, and to let him know that Kong's will left the apartment and market to him. He never crossed the street or went into the building, but had watched then turned away. This time, he had no choice.

The curtain flicked again. In the dim glow of the streetlights, he could just make out part of Taibo's face. He backed into the alley and leaned against the wall of the building.

The flight had been an agonizingly long one. He was exhausted from the battle at the warehouse, the interrogation at the Police Station, Ling's death, and now the wait. The stone wall was cool on his heated skin. He took deep breaths. He had to wait. He had to do everything just right.

He'd known better than to take the taxi directly to the building where

Taibo held Monica. Instead he exited one street over and crossed through the alley. From there he was able to survey the area for the best way to reach Taibo without warning him of his coming.

He pulled his cell phone from his belt clip and dialed Captain Arama's cell phone. Arama answered immediately.

"It's Tao," Tao said.

"Where are you, Wong?" Arama demanded, snatching a black marker pen and writing the address in big letters as Tao gave it to him. He held up the pad of paper where his men could see it. They grabbed jackets, guns, and badges and headed out the door.

"Listen to me," Tao," Arama said as he stormed out of his office. "Wait for backup. Understand? No heroics. We're on our way. Linden is almost there. Don't do anything until we've arrived. I mean it."

Tao didn't answer.

"Wong!"

There was no answer and the phone disconnected. Arama cursed as he climbed into his car and barked at his driver to get moving.

Lee and Patrick left the airport at a dead run and knocked a businessman out of the way to jump into the first available taxi. Lee gave the driver the address to the police station and they arrived a few minutes later. Lee explained who he was and a short time later he and Patrick were in the back of a squad car speeding to the address Tao had given to Arama. Lee spoke briefly to Arama via the cell phone and was told exactly where Tao had gone.

Lee closed his eyes and tried to calm his jangled nerves.

"Everything's come together," he said to Patrick. "In a full circle. I should've been there for him. I've let him down."

"Lee," Patrick said, "you know that's not right. These are his demons not yours."

Lee stared at his reflection in the window of the car. There were deep furrows between his brows. He knew Patrick was right, but it didn't make it any easier.

Tao clipped the phone back onto his belt and returned to the entrance of the alley. Taibo was still at his post, still waiting.

It would take the police time to reach them. He wanted them there, for Monica's sake. But he wasn't going to wait for them.

He slipped into the alley and made a rebounding leap against one wall to reach the fire escape ladder above him. With the agility of a monkey, he was up the ladder and on the roof of the building situated diagonally from the apartment building. He moved to the far end of the roof and launched himself to the next roof six feet away.

Safely across, he took time to calm his nerves, breathe, and repeat the jump to the next building. Three buildings away from the alley, he slipped to the ground, passed through the alley between the buildings and climbed the ladder in the back to the roof of the apartment. His soft-soled shoes made little sound as he crossed to the door from the roof to the apartment below. It took him a few seconds to pick the lock on the door and ease onto the dark stairs.

Taibo was growing restless. His breathing grew louder. His hands twitched on the fabric of the curtain. With a snarl, he dropped it and turned on Monica. In three strides he was at her side and backhanded her, taking his fury out on her because she was the only one handy.

She whimpered from the pain as he grabbed her hair and pulled her upright then slapped her again. An ugly gash on her cheek bled under the gag into her mouth. The taste of blood made her want to vomit.

"Where is he?" Taibo demanded. "Why isn't he here?"

Monica shook her head. She didn't know and prayed Tao wouldn't come.

"Stop sniveling," he said.

He brought his hand up as if to strike her again. She did her best not to flinch, to meet his eyes and keep her shoulders straight. He turned away.

"Be brave," he said. "Show me how strong you are. It won't last."

With an ugly laugh, he turned to the curtain, his rifle forgotten on the chair by the table.

The door to the apartment burst open. Taibo whirled around as Monica kicked the rifle out of the chair. It went skidding across the floor too far for him to reach.

"I'm here," Tao said in answer to Taibo's question.

Taibo gauged the distance to the rifle. He didn't see a gun in Tao's hands or anywhere on him, but that didn't mean he was unarmed.

"Go ahead," Tao said.

"And what will you do?" Taibo said.

Tao said nothing. As on the roof of the warehouse, he let his silence have its unnerving effect.

"You think you're going to frighten me," Taibo said, "but you're wasting your time. I've been waiting on you, knew you would come. Now it's you and me, little cousin, and I'm not going to lose."

"Turn her loose," Tao said. "then it will be just you and me. She has nothing to do with us."

Taibo laughed.

"But everything to do with you," he said, "and I intend to dispose of everything that has to do with you."

"Ling is dead," Tao said. "Her father, husband, and husband's father, Uncle Kai Chi; but it was Kim who killed them, including Mama and Ba ba. Not you. You're nothing."

"You can't stop me, Tao," Taibo said. "I'm going to put you away, but before I do, you'll see your wife taken from you, just like Uncle Kim took your mother. You know where you are. I didn't choose this place by accident.

Taibo held Tao's gaze and inched towards the rifle. Tao's eyes never left him.

"There aren't any ghosts here, Taibo," Tao said.

Taibo was almost within reaching distance of the rifle.

"You touch that gun," Tao said, "and I will kill you."

"You can't," Taibo said. "You don't have it in you to kill in cold blood. Uncle Kim knew. You thought you were such a tough cop, but you're not a killer."

Tao's mind flashed back to Arturo Gravelli. Not a killer? He wasn't so sure.

"You killed Kim," he said. "the man you worshiped, or have you forgotten who fired the gun, Taibo?"

Taibo sprang for the rifle. Tao was faster and met him with a flying twist and leap that landed in the middle of Taibo's chest and sent him crashing into the table behind him.

Coughing, Taibo pulled himself to his feet and the two men faced each other with all of their hatred showing.

Taibo charged, his fists raining blows that Tao parried with equal skill. He found his opening and drove his elbow into Taibo's ribs. Taibo bent, and barely avoided the knee that would've driven his nose into his head. He plowed into Tao, pinned his arms to his sides and wrapped his leg around Tao's knees.

Tao planted his feet firmly on the floor and locked his joints to avoid being toppled. With a heave and a yell, he threw Taibo away and slammed his fist into his face.

Blood spurted from a deep cut on Taibo's brow. Roaring he came at Tao, managing to duck under his fists. He hit him around the waist and locked his arms. With a twist, he lifted Tao and squeezed. They both heard the snap of a rib before he threw Tao against the floor.

Monica tried to scream, afraid that Tao was hurt, but he used his position to his advantage. His legs whipped around Taibo's ankles and knocked him from his feet. He spun and pushed from his shoulders, landing upright. He kicked, but Taibo rolled away from the blow and regained his feet.

Both men were bloodied and covered in sweat and dust. Both of them breathed hard but neither was willing to give an inch. This battle would be the finale and only one would walk away.

Taibo grabbed Tao again and threw him against the wall. Tao felt the air rush out of his lungs and a stab of pain shot through his back. Momentarily paralyzed, he couldn't avoid Taibo's next blow. The hard fist drove deep into Tao's ribcage and again into his stomach. He yelled at the pain as the newly broken rib stabbed his lung.

Monica struggled to pull the ropes from her wrists. Her arms bled where the ropes rubbed her skin raw. She was desperate to help Tao. If she could only get loose and get to the gun, she could stop Taibo. When Tao hit the wall, she screamed "no" but her cry was muffled by the gag. She could see Tao had hit the damaged part of his back. He couldn't fight back and she was afraid that Taibo would kill him.

In the distance she heard the approaching sirens. She kicked her feet trying to dislodge the ropes that held her ankles. One foot finally slipped free and she ran to the window.

"Hurry," she urged silently as she tried to dislodge the gag using the window frame. She finally dragged it away from her mouth.

Taibo heard the sirens as well and let his guard drop for just a second, long enough for Tao to drive clamped fists into his chest. Taibo stumbled and crashed into a chair that broke with his weight. He hit the floor with a thud and his head struck the edge of the table on the way down. He was out.

Breathing hard, Tao went to Monica and untied her. She wrapped her arms around his neck and clung to him. He held her tight for a moment then gently released her.

"Let me tie him up," he said.

The flashing lights careened through the apartment. She heard men shouting and running feet. It was a relief. She turned to tell Tao, but the words never left her lips. Instead she screamed as Taibo, on his feet, aimed his rifle at Tao who stood between them.

"I told you, little cousin," Taibo said. "I won't lose."

Chapter 38

Tao heard the click of the hammer but by the time it was released, he was moving. He kicked high and knocked the rifle out of Taibo's hands. It fired, rebounded off of the wall, and fell to the floor, discharging again.

The shouts grew louder, more urgent as the police, hearing the shots, ran to the apartment.

Tao was on Taibo, pinning him against the wall, his strong hands locked around Taibo's throat. Taibo pummeled his fists against Tao's arms, but couldn't break the hold. He kicked, but Tao turned and the kicks landed on his thighs and shins.

"Tao, let go," a voice commanded from behind them.

He only half heard it through the roar of blood in his ears.

"Tao! Let go now."

He heard the click of a gun. He released his grip from Taibo's neck and slowly dropped his hands to his sides.

"Now move away," Linden ordered.

Tao stepped back, his eyes riveted on Taibo's face. Linden motioned two officers towards Taibo.

"Cuff him," he said.

The two officers started forward, pulling their cuffs as they went. Before they reached him, Taibo propelled his body away from the wall and knocked them into Linden and Tao. Before the men could untangle themselves, he wrapped his arms around Monica's neck and was backing towards the window. Monica scratched at his arms with her nails and kicked his knees and ankles, but was unable to break his iron grip.

Tao watched him, his eyes slit as a low gutteral growl left his throat. It was not a human sound.

"Let her go, Taibo," Linden ordered. "You've nowhere to run."

182

"Yes I do," Taibo said.

He shoved a chair in the way of an advancing Tao and dragged Monica to the window. Tao pushed past the chair and reached for her, but Taibo spun her out of his reach and threw her out. Her scream was cut short as she hit the street below.

Before Taibo could follow her, Tao was on him. Hands tried to restrain his but this time he didn't relinquish his grip as he slammed Taibo's head against the wall. As Linden's men pulled Tao away, Taibo ducked out of their reach. Tao jerked free from the officer holding him and went after Taibo, catching him in the middle of the room. Taibo threw a right punch, missed as Tao evaded the blow and kicked Taibo in the midsection. Taibo tripped, stumbled against the bed, lost his balance and fell against the open window. Tao made a grab for him, but was a second too late. The window frame and glass disintegrated as Taibo fell, his arms windmilling, to the pavement below.

A second later, Linden's men had Tao face against the wall, his arms jerked behind him as he was handcuffed. He was turned to face the officers who held him there as Linden shouted orders into his radio.

Tao was breathing hard, each breath a knife thrust in his left lung as the rib pressed against it. Linden was speaking to him, or he thought it was Linden. His eyesight blurred as he fought the pain. He couldn't hear anything through the roaring in his ears. He was led from the apartment to the street where he was met by an angry Captain Arama.

Arama's car arrived as Linden's team stormed the apartment. The squad car with Lee and Patrick slid to a stop behind it. They had just reached Arama when they heard the scream and turned to see Monica falling from the window. She dropped onto the old canvas awning over the market door, bounced, and landed safely in Lee's arms as he ran to get under her. They both fell, his body cushioning hers. Sitting on the sidewalk, he held her close as she sobbed hysterically into his shoulder.

Patrick knelt next to them, his hand on Lee's shoulder.

"You okay, pal?" he asked.

Lee nodded. Then came the shout and another falling body. This one missed the awning and landed sprawled on its back on the pavement. Police officers ran to the man but it was too late.

Lee couldn't see who it was. He looked to Patrick who went to see and returned with the news it was Taibo.

"His skull is caved in," he said in a whisper. "He's dead."

Lee nodded again. He said nothing. He cradled Monica closer. Taibo deserved what he got.

Patrick touched his shoulder. He looked up in time to see Linden leading a handcuffed Tao into the street. Arama quickly moved to Tao's side, blocking Lee's view.

"Pat, find out why he's in cuffs," Lee said. "What happened."

Tao's face was white, his eyes vacant as Arama met him next to the squad car.

"Tao," Arama said, "Tao, she's alive. Lee is with her. The awning broke her fall."

His words didn't register. Tao didn't acknowledge.

"Let's go," Linden said and gently guided him to the car.

"Linden," Arama said. "Take it easy. Tell the infirmary to take a look at him."

Linden got into the back seat with his silent prisoner.

Patrick took that time to pull Arama aside to ask what was going on.

Lee watched them leave. His first duty was to Monica, but he thought Tao should've been taken to the hospital, not to the police station.

The ambulance arrived and Monica was gently lifted onto the stretcher and placed inside. He climbed in with her, as did Patrick. Patrick explained the situation as the attendant checked Monica's vital signs. He announced everything was stable. The rest of the ride to the hospital was in silence, Monica's hand held tightly in Lee's.

Tao was escorted by Linden to Arama's office. Linden asked him if he wanted anything. He shook his head, his gaze on his folded hands in his lap. Linden moved outside the door to wait.

Tao was arrested for obstructing justice and withholding evidence. He didn't know if Monica was alive, safe, hurt, or worse. Vaguely, he remembered somone said something about her, but his mind hadn't registered it.

He heard Linden shift his stance, the only sound other than his own breathing. After what seemed like hours, Captain Arama entered his office and sat behind his desk. Tao felt his eyes on him, but didn't look up.

"I've been in a meeting with the Chief, the Commissioner, the IA, and the DA," Arama said. "I've explained the circumstances to them. Bryson Royo just arrived from Hong Kong and testified on your behalf, as did Lee and Patrick Swayne."

He waited. Tao's posture never changed.

"They've decided, after a lot of deliberation, to drop all charges and release you."

He watched, but still there was no reaction.

"What you did was way out of line. You know that."

Tao's response was a heavy sigh.

Arama leaned forward, his elbows on his desk, his hands clenched in front of him.

"Tao, you know what you did was wrong."

Though his chin remained down, Tao lifted his eyes to Arama.

"I know that creep was responsible for the death of a lot of people you cared about, and between you and me, he got what he had comin', but you're a cop, first and foremost. You're too good a cop to lower yourself to vigilantism."

Tao's gaze never wavered. After a long silence, Arama continued.

"You've been under a lot of stress since the shooting last year. Your head injury caused a lot of problems. You were under extreme duress in this situation. Grief for your Uncle, fear for your wife, concern for Bryson who'd just been shot."

Tao knew Arama was telling him what the official report would say. It would justify the decision of his superiors.

"As of today," Arama said, "your disability discharge is official. You're off the force, full pension and so on—but..."

He sighed and shook his head.

"They want you out of the country."

Tao straightened.

"It isn't right," Arama said, before he could say anything. "You were the victim, from what I hear, for a very long time. The DA would revoke your citizenship if he could. But your records speaks for you. So does the Constitution. Even he knows it would be more than his career is worth to pursue anything that stupid."

Tao relaxed but only a little.

"This isn't your home," Arama said. "Not any more. Hong Kong is where you were born, where your heart's always been. Even I know that. You need to go home. Be with people who care about you. Part of what you've been looking for was there. You've settled it. Put it behind you."

Tao was amazed. He couldn't recall Arama ever sounding so paternal towards anyone. Usually he was screaming at the top of his voice, especially at him.

"What about Monica?" he asked.

"I imagine she'll return with you," Arama said.

Tao closed his eyes as the relief flooded over him.

"She's okay, Tao," Arama said. "Didn't you hear me tell you she's alive?"

Tao shook his head. The oath that came from Arama opened his eyes. Arama was already on the phone.

"Linden," he said, "I want a car out in front 10 minutes ago."

He slammed the receiver down and stood.

"Come on," he said.

Tao stifled a smile as he stood. This was the Captain Arama he knew.

In the car, Arama said, "You're not a cop here, but Superintendent Tang tells me that despite your disobeying orders, he was impressed and wants you on his Special Task Force. He knows what happened here. We spoke on the phone earlier. It made him more determined to have you on his team."

He laughed. "He doesn't know what he's asking."

Tao was dubious. That wasn't the impression Tang left him with at their last encounter. He was beginning to question Tang's judgement.

He wasn't sure what to think or do. His superiors wanted him out of their hair permanently. He'd given them plenty of trouble over the years with the way he did things. They couldn't throw him out of the country if he didn't want to go. He was a citizen, but he was also a citizen of Hong Kong. He'd grown up in the United States. He'd never really known Hong Kong even though he'd spent the first 12 years of his life there. It was the same dilemma he'd faced after the shooting. He didn't know which way to turn.

"Tao," Arama said. "We're here."

Slowly Tao extricated his tired body out of the car and straightened his protesting muscles. His sore rib stabbed him.

He followed Arama to Monica's room. She was asleep. The bruises on her face made him wince. He didn't want to wake her. She might not want to see her. If not for him, she wouldn't be there now, in the hospital, battered, bruised—he sat in the chair next to the bed and took her hand in his. He watched her, thankful she was alive.

He hadn't meant for Taibo to die. He'd meant only to arrest him, to let the police take him. But when Taibo threw Monica out of the window, all the years of training and restraint abandoned him. In that moment, he had wanted Taibo dead. If Taibo hadn't fallen, Tao wasn't too sure he wouldn't have thrown him out of the window.

He gingerly fingered his ribs. He hadn't told anyone about it. He knew he should have it looked after, but at that moment it wasn't important. The only thing that mattered to him was Monica. He leaned his head on the crisp white sheets of the bed, her hand still in his. He closed his eyes and held her hand to his cheek. He was so tired—so tired.

"When did this happen? Why wasn't this treated immediately?"

Tao was jolted awake by the voices that wormed their way into his subconscious. He opened his eyes directly into a bright light above him.

He was no longer sitting by Monica's bed, but lying on an examination table in an emergency cubicle, stripped to his shorts, with a light sheet covering his lower body. His upper torso was explosed. A doctor stood next to the table, pointing out an x-ray to a disgruntled Arama.

"We didn't know," Arama said. "He's a closed-mouth son-of-a…"

He noticed Tao's eyes were open. The doctor turned.

"You should have told someone about your injury, young man," he said. "That rib could easily have pierced your lung."

"How did you find out?" Tao asked, trying to sit up.

Arama pushed him back and pinned him with one beefy hand on his shoulder.

"Don't move," he said. "That's an order."

"Your wife's nurse found you unconscious in your wife's room," the doctor said. "Your captain told us about the fight. We felt checked you out. You've a nasty bruise on your ribcage, so I took some x-rays. Good thing I did."

"It'll heal," Tao said, shoving Arama's hand away.

"It'll go right into your lung, young man," the doctor said, "at the slightest wrong move. I've set up surgery. It'll be a few minutes. This rib is scraping the outer wall of your lung and we need to get it away from there before the worst happens."

"No," Tao said.

"Shut up," Arama said. "You're still in my custody, remember."

He turned to the doctor.

"I warn you, Doc, he's a pain-in-the-ass patient in the best of times. This isn't one of them."

The curtain to the cubicle swung to the side and a gurney arrived. Tao glared at the attendants and the doctor who gently lifted him onto it. He didn't have the strength to fight them. He hurt all over and every breath sent an electric shock through him. He knew it wouldn't matter anyway. Arama would have him restrained if he had to.

As he wheeled past the Captain, Arama winked at him. Tao sighed in resignation and stared at the lights passing overhead. He concentrated on Monica and nothing else until the anesthesia closed the black curtain over his mind.

Bright sunlight streamed into his room as the nurse flung open the curtains. She came to the end of the bed to check his chart.

"I thought I told you I didn't want to see you here again," she said.

"*Dui m jue.* I couldn't stay away."

"He speaks!" she said. "I didn't think you knew how."

She moved to his side to take his pulse and blood pressure.

"You know, you're my favorite patient."

"Oh sure," he said. "They only sent you because they know I'm scared of you."

Nurse Sharon McNeil laughed as she sat on the edge of his bed. She took his hand in hers. He didn't pull away. Instead, his fingers closed over hers. She studied their hands.

"You know," she said, "you were the worst patient I'd ever come across."

"I'm trying to change," he said.

"The man can joke," she said. "And I love that smile. Where were you hiding it all those months ago?"

"In a treasure chest a long way from here," he said.

"I saw your wife," she said. "She's worried about you."

"Really?"

"Tao Wong! You should be ashamed of yourself. She asked about you as soon as she woke and found out you're a patient. It didn't seem to surprise her though."

She lifted his chin so their gazes met.

"She's fine and so is the baby. You'll be…"

"Baby?" He tried to sit up. Pain shot through his ribs and he fell back. "What baby?"

"Your baby," Sharon said. "Monica is pregnant. Didn't she tell you?"

He shook his head.

"How long?" he asked.

"She's about two months along," Sharon said. "I can't believe she hasn't said anything. Surely you noticed?"

He shook his head.

"Men!" she said. "How could you not notice?"

"How would I know?" he asked. "I've never had a pregnant wife before. I've never been around babies for that matter."

"Do you want to see her?" Sharon asked.

"I think the question is does she want to see me?" he said.

"Tao!"

"It's a stupid question," he said.

He was worried about her, even moreso now he knew she was going to have a baby—his baby.

"I'll be right back," Sharon said.

He blinked as it sank in. His baby—their baby. He was going to be a father. And Taibo had almost taken that from him. His closed his eyes and fought the anger. He'd have to let it go, let the anger go, for the sake of his son…or daughter.

Sharon patted him gently on the shoulder. "Hey," she said.

He opened his eyes. Monica was parked in a wheelchair next to his bed. The bruises on her face weren't so dark, but were still ugly. It hurt him to see them. Even so, to him she was still beautiful.

Sharon left them, giving him a little wave from the door.

"Should you be up?" Tao asked, tracing a finger down Monica's cheek.

"I'm fine," she said. "Just shook up, a few bruises."

"I thought," he said, "when you went out the window, I thought…"

"Something broke my fall," she said. "I think it was Lee."

She laughed. He managed a smile. Arama had told him in the car about the awning and Lee's miraculous catch.

"Is he okay?" he asked.

"He was here this morning," she said. "He said he's sore, but he's okay. He came to see you but you were asleep and he didn't want to wake you up."

They were silent a moment.

"Why didn't you tell me," he asked, "about the baby?"

She frowned and pretended to pout.

"I was saving that for our anniversary," she said. "It's next week, remember."

She caressed his face. Her fingers were soft and smelled like soap.

"I can hardly believe it's been a year. So much has happened, and then with all that's been going on, I forgot to tell you. I guess I'll have to give you something else."

He shook his head.

"You're all I need, you and our baby."

She leaned forward and kissed him.

"We're a pair aren't we," she said. "I'm sorry, Tao."

"For what?"

"For doubting you. For not believing in you."

She smoothed his hair from his forehead.

"For being angry with you instead of understanding. For not being more careful after you warned me to."

He placed the palm of his hand against her cheek.

"Love me forever," he said.

She kissed him. He wrapped his arms around her.

"I was holding too tight to the wrong things," he said. "To the past, to my fear, to my anger. I am so sorry."

"I love you forever, Tao Wong," she said. "We'll go home, to Hong Kong. You and Lee will start your business again and we'll all look ahead and let the past go. I know about the offer from the Hong Kong police. That's up to you. I'll be at your side either way."

He shook his head.

"That was yesterday," he said with conviction, "but not tomorrow. I don't want that life anymore."

Their kiss was deep and binding. She tickled his ear.

"Don't do that," he said. "You know what happens when you do that."

Smiling coyly at him, she got into the bed and snuggled close to him.

"I do," she whispered as she kissed his cheek. "but I'll wait until your rib is better."

He laughed. To hold her would be enough—until then.

Printed in the United States
131672LV00006B/7-12/P